THEY lay huddled in the darkness of the cabin.

"Sam?"

"It's all right. We have to stay here."

"For how long?"

"Until dawn."

She was silent.

"Get out of your wet clothes," Durell suggested. "I'm going to do the same. I have to dry my gun, too."

They stripped in silence. Sam found some rice and a bottle of wine. "A picnic," he grinned.

They crouched side by side. "I'm cold, Sam," whispered Pala Mir. It was stifling in the cabin.

"It's just the shock," he told her.

"You are a strange man, Sam Durell," she said.

"Why?"

"Don't you want me. Here we are, alone, naked. . . ."

"Yes. I want you."

She laughed. "But you think I would be better off if I slept and rested."

Sam did not answer.

"Do you think I am young and beautiful?"

"Yes."

"Could you not love me—a little?"

Sam was only human.

ASSIGNMENT—

WHITE RAJAH

Edward S. Aarons

A FAWCETT GOLD MEDAL BOOK

Fawcett Publications, Inc., Greenwich, Conn.
Member of American Book Publishers Council, Inc.

ASSIGNMENT—

WHITE RAJAH

DURELL ran and fell and picked himself up and ran again.

He had been running for a lifetime, perhaps half an hour, and he did not want to stop and kill them. It was better to try to escape. There had been enough killing here.

In the darkness of the jungle, inland from the beach, he did not know if it was night or day. He did not raise his head to look at the treetops. They might be there, in the branches, waiting to pick him off, but he couldn't do anything about that.

The jungle steamed. Vines, creepers, and obscene green things picked and clawed at him, tripped him and slashed at him. He splashed through ankle-deep water, then waded knee-deep, feeling the muck underfoot, ignoring it. He pushed on. Now and then he heard them, hurrying after him.

He judged he was no more than five hundred yards from the river, but it was invisible, of course, and he wasn't sure now if he hadn't circled completely. Perhaps the river was to his right and perhaps it was to his left.

He ran on.

He had been on the beach, an idyll of white sand and emerald water, leaning coconut palms and chattering monkeys. The tanker in the bay was anchored well offshore, away from the riots that smoked in the city. He had simply been waiting for the time to meet Chiang Gi when they came at him, silently and swiftly, mad-eyed, their knives gleaming in the setting sun.

The worst of it was that there was nothing personal in their lust to kill him. It was part of the insanity that had erupted in the city, pulling out mobs of screaming Malays and angry Chinese, bursting into fires that took parts of the Chungsu section of the city, leaving behind bodies and overturned vehicles, pedicabs and buses, smashed and looted shops. The riots smoldered and leaked blood, gasoline, and oil in the fine, palm-lined avenues.

It had been going on for two days. Durell had arrived in the middle of it.

And now, somewhere above the thudding of his heart, he heard sudden, rolling thunder, and with the abrupt habit of tropical climates, it began to rain.

He suddenly knew he could run no farther.

He came out on a path, turned right, and slowed to a walk. Then he drew out his gun and held it loosely in his hand, his right arm dangling, his left hand pushing aside a vine that had grown almost overnight across the path. A great banyan tree loomed ahead, and although he heard the patter and drive of the rain on the treetops above, it hadn't yet penetrated down through the leafy green levels to the ground.

It was almost dark.

Durell stopped and put his back against one of the vast roots of the banyan and looked down the path.

They were coming.

He felt no hatred toward them. They certainly did not know him. They merely wanted to kill, as they had been killing for two days now.

The consulate windows had all been smashed. The library was burned. The compound walls had been daubed with paint and oil and blood. One of the Malay girls who worked as a typist had been caught in the street and torn apart into bloody pieces of flesh. A Chinese secretary, a mild-mannered young man, had been beheaded at the consulate gates. David Condon, the consul, had ordered Durell out of the city and out of the province. Durell couldn't go, of course. His orders were very explicit about that.

He drew a deep breath, leaned harder against the banyan root, and watched the path. A minute went by. The shadows were very black now; it was almost night. The rain pattered lower down through the leaves, and he felt the heavy, warm drops on his head, his face, his shoulders.

Two men appeared suddenly in the path, not very far from him.

They looked at him with surprise.

"American?" one called.

"Yes," Durell said.

"What you do here?"

"I go to see Pala Mir."

"Ha ha."

"It is the truth."

"Pala Mir sees no one."

"She will see me."

The second man said, "It is dangerous here for strangers."

"Yes, I know."

"You are sure you are American?"

"Yes, I'm sure."

They were Malays, and in ordinary times, before the racial madness struck the city, they would have been selling vegetables or working their rice paddies and laughing. The two men still hefted their long parangs with indecision. The rain came down harder now, wet the blades, and made little shining rivulets along the cutting edges.

"You have a gun," the first Malay said. "Why do you run from us?"

"I thought you wanted to kill me," Durell said.

"We were mistaken."

"I have no quarrel with you," Durell said.

"Do you have a quarrel with Pala Mir?"

"No."

"She will not see you."

"Then I will return to the city."

"It is dangerous," said the Malay.

"All of life is dangerous."

"That is true. Many people have died lately. Very well, American, you may go."

"Which way is the river?" Durell asked.

"You were going the right way. Keep on."

"Thank you," Durell said.

They nodded, put away their knives, and abruptly melted into the jungle, gone as suddenly as they had appeared. For several minutes Durell did not move from his safe vantage point at the banyan tree. He knew there had been more of them, more than just those two. Durell was trained to be careful. It was a cardinal rule for survival in his business.

When ten minutes had gone by and there was no further sign of the men who had pursued him, he left the shelter of the banyan tree and walked on up the path to the river.

2

THE river channel was not the main channel that came down to the coast at Pasangara and poured sluggishly into this last green reach of the South China Sea. This was delta country, and a hundred river beds divided and met and divided again, forming swampy islands, jungles, deadfalls of broken trees and rotting vegetation alive with insects, reptiles, and animal life. Only from the top of the new, towering, white government building in Pasangara itself, provincial capital of this semiautonomous state, could the dim mountains be seen, folding and refolding along the spine of the Malay Peninsula.

Durell found the hut in the waning tropical daylight. The rain thundered, hissed, and banged on the tin roof, rattling like an old Gatling gun, pouring and chuckling down the sides of the hut and onto the wooden pier where Chiang Gi should have been waiting with his boat.

Chiang Gi was not here. He was ten minutes late.

Durell looked up and down the river, walked out on the rickety dock, and looked under the slatted boards. Then he went back to the hut to get out of the rain.

The old man should have been here.

He felt chilly now in his linen suit that was much the worse for wear after his run through the jungle. He would not have worn it except for a warning from the young, earnest consul, David Condon, that he would have to impress Pala Mir if he wanted to get anywhere with her. He decided ruefully that he could hardly impress anyone at the moment.

Durell had put away the snub-nosed .38 S & W under his linen suit; it was a weapon not quite approved by General Dickinson McFee. Durell could use his hands, fingers, anything that came into his grip, if needed, but McFee had said there would be few problems. His stay was really an R & R after his recent trip to Peking. Durell had his doubts about it.

The hut stood on stilts above the water, and from under it through the creaking floorboards came the smells of primeval mud and rotting things and, oddly, a scent of charcoal smoke. Equally at odds with these surroundings, he heard the dim iron pealing of convent bells, like a faraway, dream-like echo drifting down the placid, muddy river. Chiang Gi had assured him, crossing himself— he had been converted by an earnest Dominican sixty years ago—that no one ever came to this hut, and his presence here would not be noticed.

Durell doubted this, too.

It was his business to be skeptical. It was the best way to stay alive.

Chiang Gi was now fifteen minutes late.

The river was utterly dark. There was no moon. Durell took a pencil flash from his rain-soaked coat and considered the hut. There were no lamps, no furniture except a broken-legged table and two stools. There had once been a fire in the hut, and part of the plaited reed wall had burned away. He was thinking about this when he heard Chiang Gi tie up at the lopsided dock.

"Mr. Durell?"

The old Malay's voice boomed like a foghorn.

"Speak softly, my friend," Durell said.

Chiang Gi grunted. "I am not a superstitious man, sir, but I like to speak louder than the ghosts."

"Is this place haunted?"

"Ah, you feel their presence?"

"I feel something," Durell said.

"The black of the tomb, the bite of the sea. No one living can hear us." Chiang Gi's stained old teeth shone in the gloom. "Everyone in this area is afraid of the place. Did I forget to tell you?"

"I don't think you forgot."

"Ah, well. The Holy Mother protects us. I am a devout man ever since Father Donaldson instructed me. Old ghosts cannot frighten me—much. Long ago, some fishermen and a boy used this house; the boy was their cook and stayed here while the men went to sea. One day, they picked up a body, a drowned man. They brought him back, left the corpse in their boat, and teased the boy, telling him they had an extra mouth to feed and to go kick the man awake who was lying in the boat. The boy did so, being obedient, and came back to set another place at that table, saying the stranger was coming. And then the fishermen heard the wet footsteps come up from the river, where my boat is now tied up, and the dead man walked in here and sat at the table, where the rice was ready and hot. He was all green and swollen with water and half-eaten by sharks. The fishermen were struck dead with fright, and only the boy was left alive to row to Pasangara and tell the tale. Ever since, no one comes here."

"When did this happen?"

"Five, six years ago. So we are safe here."

"Are we safe from Pala Mir?"

"Ah, that is another tale," Chiang Gi said.

"Can we see her this evening?"

"Everything is upset. The riots. Martial law. A curfew has been declared, did you know?"

"No," Durell said.

"The killing is senseless. And I, who am half-Chinese and half-Malay, what am I to do? Everyone is my enemy tonight."

"Not I," said Durell.

"I hope not," said the boatman. "As for the young ranee, although, of course, no one really uses that title for her any more, or for her brother, or for the old grandfather, who was the White Rajah in the bad old days of oppression and colonialist, imperialist occupation and exploitation—"

"Cut the nonsense," Durell said. He was listening to something else—a small sound, high in the sky, far to the northeast over the sea.

"I apologize. You Americans are so sensitive."

"You work for us, don't you?"

Chiang Gi shrugged. "The money is good. The work is very easy. Yes, I work for you. But as for Pala Mir, she is young and beautiful and unpredictable. An evil woman, some say. A witch, some think. She may have changed her mind."

"But she is expecting me," Durell objected. He was still listening. The small sound was larger now.

"Pala Mir and her brother and her grandfather are allowed to live here only on sufferance of our new democracy," Chiang Gi said. He shrugged his slender shoulders. He was a fisherman of Pasangara. His thick hair was pure white, and his brown face reflected the best of his mixed ancestry. He smelled of spices and rice, and Durell liked him and felt secure with him.

Durell said suddenly, "Do you have my bag?"

"In the boat, *tuan*."

Durell started running. He ran out onto the rickety dock and almost broke an ankle when a rotten plank gave way under him. After he was in the boat with its new, gleaming outboard motor, he tore the zipper open and took out the radio transceiver, a powerful, miniaturized device that the lab boys had built in the basement at No. 20 Annapolis Street in Washington, which was the headquarters for K Section.

He flicked the switch and put the tiny earphone to his ear and tuned it as best he could, using the pencil flash from his pocket. Something splashed violently in the water nearby. The rain had stopped, and there was a hot humid wind blowing in from the sea, across the delta, and up the river.

The sound in the sky was a growing roar, a massive thunder, and he could spot them both, two navigation lights twinkling high up in the sky, but not too high. They were lowering, as if for a descent.

He marked their direction with a pocket compass: south by southwest. He knew the sound of the jet engines, those enormous propulsion units of unique design. He had studied them for hours before his flight here.

The jets were Thrashers, TDY-4's.

They did not belong here. They belonged aboard a certain aircraft hundreds of miles north and east, beyond Saigon, where a war was going on.

"Chiang Gi, did you ever hear or see planes like that before?"

"No, sir. Is the government sending them down because of the rioting in Pasangara?"

"I doubt it."

They were U. S. Navy planes, and they were lost, and heading farther and farther away from the aircraft carrier they called home. They had no business here. They were violating neutral territory.

He heard a crackling in his tiny earphone.

"How much longer, Four-Ten? I'm about out. Over."

"Roger. Forty-two seconds. Maintain silence."

"Where in hell are we?"

"Coming home, buddy, coming home. Shut up."

The voices were as American as apple pie. But Durell knew that one of the voices was an impostor.

The two planes thundered overhead and faded away, maintaining course, speed, and altitude. The air shook for a moment, then grew quieter, and the parrots and monkeys began shrieking curses at the sky for disturbing them. Durell snapped down the antenna, repacked the receiver, and put it back in the boat. Chiang Gi stared at the southwest.

Durell said, "Let's go."

He wished General McFee had told him more about this job.

3

THE American consul to Pasangara, David Condon, had met Durell at the airport reluctantly, thirty-six hours earlier. Condon was an earnest young man with hair a bit too long, distinct sunglasses, and a shirt worn outside his fine Brooks Brothers slacks. He also wore sandals, no socks, and his ankles were dirty with the red dust of the delta soil.

"I really can't see why you are here. It's a bad time, you know. Really dreadful. They started rioting just this morning, killing each other, burning shops, looting. The consulate is under rather heavy guard, and there's word out that Premier Kuang may call for a curfew."

"Very distressing," Durell said.

"May I ask if Washington sent you here because of the riots?"

"No, you may not ask."

"Well, really, I *am* the American consul here, and I must object—"

"Object to Washington. Do you have an employee, a second secretary named Hammond, George Hammond?"

"Well, yes, but—"

"I'm here to consult with him," Durell said.

"Hammond? Poor old George? But I can't see—"

"You don't have to," Durell said.

The Cadillac was air-conditioned, and so was the consulate, new and modern, pristine white in immaculate green lawns and shrubbery. Pasangara, however, had gone mad. Smoke boiled up from the Chungsu area, near the docks, where most of the Chinese lived. Someone threw a rock through the rear window of Condon's lovely Cadillac, and the air-conditioning became useless. When they arrived at the consulate after pushing through mobs of screaming, violent Malays, they found that the consulate's air-conditioning was also useless because the rioters had managed to demolish the vast expanses of glass in the building's facade. An employee with a pale face and trembling lips let Condon and Durell in and quickly barred the gate again. The place was in a state of siege.

Half an hour later the local garrison was called out, and a company of soldiers, small and alert and armed with American weapons, rushed around the consulate to form a cordon against the mobs. They fired twice into the air and then into the crowd, the soldiers being almost engulfed by the screaming hordes that turned the boulevard into a nightmare. When two sprawled bodies testified that they meant business and the crowd still did not retreat, two minitanks rumbled up and down, threatening to smash a few more frenzied men into the hot asphalt. Only then did the rioters move elsewhere to find easier pickings among the frightened Chinese who lived in Chungsu.

Meanwhile, Durell had consulted with George Hammond.

Hammond had been with K Section, the trouble-shooting branch of the Central Intelligence Agency, for over twenty years, but like most of General McFee's long-term employees, he had not been permitted to retire. Looking at Hammond, Durell wondered if he saw his own future in the man.

At one time, Hammond had been top controller for K Section agents dealing with NATO, then had been based in Rome and, for a time, Beirut. A lean, taciturn man, it was once thought by those who were poorly informed that Hammond, hoping for eventual command of K Section, was merely playing Cassius to McFee's Caesar. It had never worked out like that. A mistake in East Germany had seen Hammond return with broken legs, a shattered hip, a concussion, a ruptured kidney, a blinded left eye, and psychic scars that reduced him to a wreck, a ghost of the man he had once been.

It happened sometimes to the best of them, Durell thought.

Because Hammond, like Durell, had been red-tabbed in the MVD files at No. 2 Dzherzinsky Square in Moscow and in Peking's Black House records, too, retirement and a return to normal civilian life were out of the question. He had spent two years being debriefed until every possible operation on which he might have had relevant data was ended. Even then, he was not permitted a normal life. He had been shunted to jobs as security officer in various embassies; then as he approached his sixties, he was gradually passed into quiet backwaters and consulates such as Pasangara.

Only chance, a turn of the dice, had brought Hammond to the surface again. He might not be prepared for it. He knew it, and Durell knew it.

"Cajun. Good to see you. You've grown older."

"Before our time," Durell said. Hammond's grip was

limp and bony. He wore his thinning hair brushed forward to hide his receding hairline. His limp was scarcely noticeable. They had done a fine prosthetic job on his blind eye. The office was a dim, damp cubby down in the lower regions of the elegant consulate building. The air-conditioning, which wasn't working this day, thanks to the shattered glass facade, wasn't even piped in. A small electric fan on a subexecutive civil service desk pushed humid air around. The desk was clear of papers. It didn't look as if Hammond had been very busy in this tropical backwater.

"I'm flattered they sent you," Hammond said.

"I'm glad to be working with you, George."

"Not much work here."

"There's going to be."

Hammond said, "I was thinking of getting married. Settling down here."

"You like Pasangara?"

"It's as good a place as any."

"Who's the woman?"

Hammond looked uncomfortable. "A local girl, Chinese. Premier Kuang's daughter, as a matter of fact. Maybe too young for me, but—" Hammond laughed. "Kuang has a lot of shops in town, and I tried to help with police protection this morning. It's all a lot of crazy shit that hit the fan, this race rioting. People will never learn."

"What started it?"

Hammond wet his lips. Durell couldn't tell the bad eye from the good. "The Chinese run the businesses and are energetic and profit-minded. The Malays are agricultural and are happy in their paddies. The Chinese grabbed too much, I guess, and some incident blew the top off. Sit down, Sam."

Durell sat down. The fan blew hot air into his face. There were no windows in the office. The place was suffocating. It was, he reflected, a syndrome of the present century that architects took no notice of nature or human failings and presumed windows unnecessary and air-conditioning infallible.

"Did you ask for the Pasangara assignment, Sam?" Hammond asked.

"No, not especially."

"I wonder if McFee forgot I was here. I sent in the original reports, you know."

"On the Thrashers?"

"Sure, the Thrashers. The Navy is in a flap. Eleven sorties mysteriously disappear, no Maydays, no claims by the Viet Cong or Hanoi, no trace of planes or pilots. I heard 'em coming over three times, so far."

"The Navy claims eleven missing, and you heard three," Durell said. "And nothing else?"

Hammond lit a thin black cigar. It didn't help the dead air in his cubbyhole of an office. He looked tired and unhappy. He looked at Durell as if he wished Durell were not there.

"It's a waste of time, Cajun. I checked it out. Nothing but my imagination, maybe." Hammond's grin was dubious. "Perhaps I merely hoped to get back into the center of things. It's been quiet here in Pasangara. I figure they'll bury me here some day."

"You're sure you heard Thrashers?" Durell persisted.

"Yes, I'm sure."

"You asked around?"

"Quietly. Cajun, don't push it. I know this business. I was in it while you were still at Yale, cracking law books and town girls."

"I know."

"And don't tell me times have changed and passed me by. Nothing really changes that much."

"George, I told you I didn't ask to be sent here."

"I could handle it myself, you know. Be a nice change from considering my constipation. All this rice ties you up sometimes." Hammond's voice was a quiet complaint. His seersucker suit was rumpled and sweat-stained. Durell wondered how it could be because there seemed to be no juice left in him at all. "I don't know what more you can do here, Sam, than I've done. I imagine you read my reports in Washington."

"In Taiwan. I was briefed there. Happened to be handy, that's all." Durell didn't know why he should be concerned with Hammond's sensitivities. "George, can't you give me any leads beyond your reports?"

"All the planes went thataway," Hammond said, and flapped a bony hand vaguely. "South–southwest, toward the mountains."

"And they didn't come back?"

"They didn't come back."

"No rumors, no fairy tales among the hill people about crashes, prisoners, American pilots wandering around?"

"Nothing."

"George, Washington wonders if it could be a ring of defectors."

"Hell," Hammond said.

"I don't believe it, either," Durell said. "But the planes and the pilots have to be somewhere. In the hills, you think?"

"That's what I think."

"Can we set up a spotting station up there?"

"Kuang won't give permission. Cites racial tensions, political instability in the province, subversives, potential guerrilla warfare, extending the Congs all the way down here. A lot of horse manure. Personally, I think it's because his daughter and I—well, anyway, no spotting station. No trips into the interior. You'd have to ask the White Rajah, if you can get him to speak coherently."

"Who is the White Rajah?"

"Old man, son of an adventurer in the '80s who set up a private principality here in the bad old days of colonialist enterprise. When he was kicked off his throne, they let him stay, him and his twin grandchildren. The boy's okay—hard-working, industrious, they say. The girl ran wild in Europe for a time, married, divorced twice, and came home recently."

"How recently?"

"A year ago."

"No connection with the Thrashers?"

"Impossible. She's in seclusion. A nut."

"How can she or her grandfather help?"

"Pala Mir owns land up in the mountains. She just might give you permission to go up there and set up a listening post. A waste of time, but that's up to you."

"Did you ask for her cooperation?"

"Couldn't get near her. But then," Hammond said grinning, "you're young and handsome, Cajun, a real tough attractive type, and you might just make it with her. Any way you like. Pala Mir is quite a dish, they say. I've never even been able to see her. You want a dossier on all the Merrydales?"

"The who?"

"Anthony Merrydale was the Englishman who became the great White Rajah of Pasangara. Fascinating history. The Malays loved him. Lots of pomp and circumstance. He married a native ranee, the blood got mixed, and the name gradually changed. It's just Mir, now. From Merrydale. They live here on sufferance. Are you really interested?"

"Yes, I'm interested," Durell said.

"All right, you'll get the dossiers. But they won't go against the provincial government's refusal to let any of us into the mountains. Where are you going to bunk?"

"The consul got me a room at the Kuan Diop Hotel."

"It's a fleabag. He's a pompous little bastard. New breed. A flit, I think."

"I'm not complaining. About this Pala Mir, how do I get to wherever she lives?"

"Chiang Gi will take you. Chiang Gi works for me. Odd jobs. The big ear. He's got sons and daughters in civil service and everywhere. You want to know anything at all about Pasangara, ask Chiang Gi."

"Sounds invaluable," Durell said.

"He is."

Hammond did not offer him a drink. He talked about his impending marriage and did not mention the missing Thrashers again. Durell was relieved when he could politely take his departure.

4

CHIANG GI seemed glad to get away from his haunted hut. The river was dark, but the rain had ended, and a foggy steam drifted over the jungle and the sluggish water. Again, Durell heard the pealing of iron convent bells. The Malay did not use his outboard motor but instead poled his way up the stream, using a single sweep at the stern. Presently a few lanterns appeared on the river bank, set on poles among thatched Dayak houses with sweeping, Polynesian-type eaves. Water purled quietly at the prow. Fishing boats were tied up at the river piers, but no one was in sight, either on the banks or in the beaten dirt streets or outside the houses. Chiang Gi twisted his pole deftly, and the shallow boat turned a sharp left into a secondary channel, slipped past sampans and native rafts, then came to a wide place in the river where an island loomed out of the misty darkness. Durell looked back at the deserted village but saw no one watching their passage.

"This is where Pala Mir lives," said Chiang.

There was a chain of sandbars, overgrown with stunted trees and lianas. Parrots squawked and something big splashed in the muddy water. A few lights gleamed ahead. To the left on the main river bank was the convent where he had heard the bells. There was a glow in the eastern sky where the moon was about to rise over the jungle.

Chiang Gi wove an erratic way among the channels to the house. It was a European-style building with a high fence around it and wide, sweeping eaves. There was a second-floor veranda above. A dog barked suddenly. There was a twist of current that turned the prow of the boat inland and, in a moment, Chiang Gi tied up to a pole on the sturdy pier. A gleaming motor launch was moored farther toward the shore.

The house was silent.

"I wish you luck with the royal lady." The old boatman grinned. "Remember, she is wicked and dangerous."

"We'll see about that."

Durell stood up in the gently rocking boat and jumped to the pier, then walked toward the gates in the wall that enclosed the massive, dim house.

George Hammond's dossiers had given him a rundown on the notorious Pala Mir, but there were contradictions in the picture. At twenty-four the young ranee had lived in the European scandal sheets for a time, appearing in the nude in underground films made by the Roman director Bardoni; she had been twice married and divorced. The first marriage was to a young Texan whose oil wells turned out to be dry. She had flown to Mexico for a divorce two months later. The second marriage was to an elderly Egyptian with villas at Montreux, Cinquaterra, and Nice. No one knew the secrets of that marriage. The Egyptian's wealth and reputation were mysteries. All that was known was a brief news item that the young ranee had been found brutally beaten and half drowned in Lac Leman, and a divorce was granted behind closed judicial doors.

The Merrydales, so many generations away from their native England, remained impoverished and pathetic figures in the Malayan province they once had ruled.

There was a twin brother who still kept his Anglo-Saxon name of Paul Merrydale and seemed to have adapted to the new order of things. He became a solid businessman of Pasangara, seemingly as good as his twin sister was depraved. Hammond's dossiers, Durell thought, were equivocal. Paul Merrydale had deplored his sister's behavior a little too strongly and publicly, it seemed. Durell preferred to draw his own conclusions.

Subject Pala Mir returned from Europe almost a year ago. Rumored she had gone to Red Belt and Moscow, no confirmation. A guest of China at Fifth International Women's Conference of Asia, remained Peking two months, frequently seen with Han Li Chao, said to be one of the five council officials of Black House.

Subject returned to Pasangara three weeks prior first Thrasher vanishment. Has lived in monastic retirement at river house ever since. Sees no one. Said to be considering entering convent. No confirmation.

Durell didn't like it. He thought Hammond was drawing unwarranted conclusions. It could be that George was too eager to get back into the field and prove he wasn't washed up. You operated in this business from solid data, a mixed bag of seemingly unrelated facts, drew conclusions, made corrections, spread a net, followed up for more data, and hoped something would come to the surface when you pulled in the bag.

Sometimes, what came to the surface could kill you.

The gate at the compound wall was locked tightly. There was no bell. Durell walked along through tall, unkempt grass and heard something slither away in the darkness. He paused and listened for the dog, but there was only an occasional twitter from the jungled river bank, the purl of the current, and the sound of the hot wind in the black trees. He looked back and saw Chiang Gi in his delicate little boat, then found a place where the wall had crumbled a bit. He jumped, caught the top, hauled himself up, and dropped down on the other side.

After all, the message from Pala Mir in reply to his note had invited him here.

Then he heard the dog growl.

He had landed in some unkempt shrubbery, and his linen suit was further torn by a probing branch. The beast came padding across the gloomy bit of lawn like some gray, yellow-eyed creature out of Asian mythology.

The animal halted, ears pricked forward, teeth bared, eyes baleful.

Then it launched itself at him without further sound.

He had time to fling up an arm and smash it across the bared fangs that snapped for his throat. The impact of the dog's weight drove him back against the garden wall. The dog fell, quickly found its feet, and came on again. Durell used his knee, chopped at the dog's throat, caught at his collar, and twisted hard. If you keep a dog trained to attack, you don't hamper it with a collar. The dog's breath squeaked and wheezed. He twisted harder, strangling it with the leather strap. Its weight seemed enormous. It fought him, sounding its enmity in the sleek throat and angry eyes until the clawing legs jerked spasmodically.

"Tatzi!"

Durell ignored the sound of the woman's voice. He held the beast down on the grass now, not relaxing his grip for an instant.

"You need not kill Tatzi," the woman said. "He will obey me."

He raised his head and saw her dim figure in the light of the doorway on the veranda. "Call him again, please."

"Tatzi?" she said.

The dying animal quivered. Durell relaxed his grip. The woman spoke in swift, fluent German, and the dog got unsteadily to its feet, flanks heaving. The woman spoke again, and the animal padded away across the grass and lay down on the veranda at her feet.

"You cannot blame Tatzi. Your entrance was unorthodox." She spoke English as fluently as her German. "You are Mr. Samuel Durell? From the American consulate?"

"You agreed to keep an appointment with me, Miss Merrydale."

"Please, call me Pala Mir. I am not English any more. I am a citizen of Pasangara."

She was beautiful. Neither European nor Asiatic, she

combined the best of both possible worlds. Her skin was
golden Malay, her eyes Chinese, her mouth and nose
English. She wore a flowered, silk sarong that clung to a
tall figure of ideal proportions. Her black hair, thick and
lustrous, was piled up in regal braids like a crown atop
her aristocratic head. The male Merrydales had chosen
their native women well. She wore no makeup, but her
mouth was full and pink, the lips soft and slightly everted.
Oddly, her eyes were a dark blue, almost matching Durell's. She wore no rings, little jewelry. The family gems,
he reflected wryly, had long gone to a pawnbroker or
had been confiscated by the new state.

"Please come in," she said.

The large chamber into which she ushered him might
once have been a provincial throne room, but now it held
all the faded gentility and shabby splendor of an epoch
of adventuring rajahs long gone by. There were no servants in sight, and he wondered if Pala Mir actually
lived here alone in the steamy melancholy of the delta
jungle. The dog lay in front of a worn Sarouk rug placed
over teak plank flooring. The yellow eyes were fixed on
Durell and never moved. He was a Doberman, out of
his climate, and the tropics didn't agree with him. (It
would have been more appropriate to see a tamed chee-
tah or leopard as a pet.) On the walls were two great
heads of Malay tigers, mounted on mahogany but moth-
eaten and seedy-looking.

The girl fixed him a drink—bourbon, Durell's pref-
erence—without asking him his choice; he wondered if
it was just a lucky guess or if she knew more about him
than he supposed. Her smile was distant, a mechanical
gesture of civility.

"I tried to send a letter to you in Pasangara, but the
riots, of course, frightened the runner. And I have no
telephone here. There was no one else to send. The
villagers have all fled, afraid of the disturbances, and the
Sisters never leave their convent down the river. It is a

pity you had your trip here for nothing. Was it dangerous?"

"Something like jaywalking in Times Square."

"I do not know New York. I never had any desire to visit it."

"Did you like Peking?" he asked.

"Ah. You Americans are so terrified of that."

"Not exactly."

"I have become tainted in your eyes merely because of my visit to the People's Republic of China?"

"Not tainted, no."

"If you think it strange," she went on, "that I live here as I do, without friends and only slight contact with Pasangaran society, I must say at once that I tolerate no personal questions, certainly none about my past, and I must request you, since Americans are usually so tactless—"

"Don't you like Americans?" he asked.

She went on, "—to refrain from any inquiries about me. It is a small miracle that my name has not been in the Continental scandal sheets for some time now. I am sure the journalists miss me, but I have no regrets and certainly do not miss them. If you wonder why I came back here, it is simply that I have come home."

She wore long, pendant jade earrings that looked antique Chinese. Her strangely dark-blue eyes in her Eurasian face regarded him with candor.

"We're off on the wrong foot," he said.

"Yes."

"I've come to ask a favor of you, that is all."

"Yes, I know about it. You wish to visit the family's old estate—the plantation, really, it's a ruin—in the mountains. You wish to stay there for a week or so?"

"That's about it."

"I cannot help you. It would be up to my brother, or my grandfather—and the provincial militia."

"I understood from your note—"

"I have changed my mind," she said flatly.

She had not asked him to sit down, and he would not

have done so, anyway. There was a generator, which supplied power and light to this island house in the river, but shadows lurked in every corner of the huge, bare room. He heard a door close softly somewhere and knew they were not alone in the house, after all. He turned slightly so that he could watch both the veranda doors and the wide French-type doors that were closed and curtained, leading into other areas of the house. The dog panted, tongue lolling, and stared at him with a promise of murder in his yellow eyes.

Pala Mir broke the momentary silence. "It is not, after all, a very pleasant time for touring the province. But then, I understand, you are not a tourist. You are really attached to the consulate?"

"Yes, but I have no immediate duties there," Durell said. "I just thought I'd—"

He saw the inner doors to the room open slightly, and when he paused, he knew his silence had forced the other man to come in openly and stop eavesdropping.

"My brother," said Pala Mir coldly, "who calls himself Paul Merrydale."

It was odd, Durell thought, that the twin sister looked Eurasian but the twin brother looked as if he had just stepped off the curb on Carnaby Street. Then he saw that the longish blond hair, carefully brushed over the tops of the ears and worn in thick, curly waves at the nape of the neck, must be dyed and that the tan was not a tan but the natural pigmentation of the skin. They looked alike in the eyes, though. The brother's might have been darker, almost black. And you don't have to be in the business long to recognize eyes that are hostile and wish you dead or, at least, far away and out of sight.

But maybe the gun prejudiced Durell. Paul Merrydale carried a beautifully chased, heavy-bored shotgun, slung loosely under a finely tailored arm of his Edwardian, wide-lapeled, white jacket. The muzzle of the shotgun was pointed casually about two inches below Durell's navel.

Durell did not bother to shake hands.

"Dear Paul," said Pala Mir, a touch of irony in her voice. "Really, your weapon is overly dramatic, don't you think? The city may be having its troubles, but nothing can bother me here. Still, it's sweet of you to be so protective."

They might have had the kind of telepathy that folklore attributes between twins, but it wasn't working.

"Who is this man? Is he the American?"

"Obviously."

"I thought you told him you would not see him."

Durell cleared his throat. He didn't like being talked about as if he weren't there. "Your sister, Mr. Merrydale, was kind enough to offer me the hospitality of your family's plantation up in the mountains. For a little vacation before I settle down to my consulate duties."

"Nonsense," Merrydale said.

"Paul—"

"Be still," he snapped at his sister. "This man is up to something. You can't trust any of these people, and our position here is delicate enough without getting involved in something that may prejudice the state's attitude toward the family. God knows, there's enough on record against us from the old man, the great White Rajah himself, even after eighty years." Merrydale didn't mind sneering at his ancestors. "I'm in business here, Pala, and on good terms with the provincial government, and they've been kind enough to leave us alone. Why should we get involved in any of this man's dirty games?"

"You're jumping to conclusions," Durell said.

"Am I?"

The challenge was obvious. It occurred to Durell that Merrydale had a pipeline into the American consulate or perhaps he was a great buddy of Consul Condon, since they liked the same hair fashions and probably spoke the same language. He wasn't sure if his cover had been blown or not, but Merrydale tipped the odds that more was known about Durell's mission than he cared to think about.

The case could be lost.

Durell said, "I'm sorry if I've intruded, then. Your pardon, Miss Pala."

Turning, he crossed the Sarouk rug under the moth-eaten tigers' heads on the wall. Paul Merrydale swung his body slightly, keeping the shotgun pointed at his belly. Durell smiled at him, then reached to catch the chased barrel and knocked it downward to the left. Twisting it, he used his other hand to chop at Merrydale's wrist, closed his fingers around the trigger, and forced the gun to go off. The explosion was shattering, echoing in the mildewed room. Merrydale was stronger than he looked. He grunted and tried to switch to the trigger of the second barrel, but Durell squeezed his fingers painfully against the metal guard until the man gasped. The shotgun came free. Durell stepped back, holding it, not taking his eyes from the other man. He emptied the second shell, pocketed it, kept the weapon broken, and tossed it to one of the Bombay chairs nearby.

"I don't like to have people pointing weapons at me," he said. "It's an old neurosis from military service."

Merrydale was pale. He smoothed his long hair, rubbed his slender, elegant hands with a handkerchief, and looked as if he wanted to wipe off the stain of Durell's touch.

"Tatzi?"

The Doberman stood up immediately. The girl said, "Tatzi is mine. Leave him alone, Paul. I am ashamed of you."

"This man can have no business with you," said Merrydale thinly. He was trying to recover his normal rate of breathing. "You were a fool to ask him here."

"I realize that now. However, he is leaving and he will go in safety. Is that clear?"

"As you say. But you and I will come to a new agreement in the future."

"I want no part of your schemes—or your partners."

Merrydale looked at her. "Be silent, darling."

"I shall be. But if you behave like this again, I just might speak to Mr. Durell once more and let him go up to the mountain house—no matter why he wants to go there."

Merrydale backed down. He knew his sister better than anyone else. He looked at Durell with a sudden smile. "I do apologize, my dear sir. It was a misunderstanding. You must be a very nervous man to imagine I threatened you with my bird gun."

"Yes, I'm always nervous," Durell said.

"Goodnight, then. Your boatman is still waiting."

Pala Mir said nothing. Glancing at her, Durell read something in her almond-shaped eyes that reflected both anger and fear. He did not think she was afraid of him or angry because of his visit here, and he decided the trip hadn't been without some gain, after all.

5

CHIANG GI sighed as Durell stepped into the little open boat. His thick white hair gleamed with beads of moisture. The night was hot and a mist curled over the river. "You were nicely entertained, *tuan?*"

"I thought you didn't care for colonialist hangovers. The term *tuan* goes back to the days of the White Rajah."

"It amuses me."

Durell sat down in the boat. "Be very careful now, Chiang. How much could you hear?"

"I heard the shot, but I was not worried about you. There was a wind, and the river was noisy."

There was no sign of a wind now, and the river was sleek and oily under the rising moon. "Don't start your motor just yet."

"I understand."

Chiang poled the little craft along the island's low shore toward the deserted fishing village. The few lights they had seen on the way up were doused now, so someone was still there. But the houses on their tall stilts above the river mud all looked dark and empty. Now and then, rickety poles slid by, marking devious channels in the delta current.

"We can cross to the Channel of Dead Men, since you are worried," the Malay suggested. "It will be safer. And I think your worry is well-founded."

Durell looked back. There was a fleck of white on the broad surface of the river, and the sound of a launch's high-powered engines. The launch carried no running lights. It would be the one he had seen tied up at Pala Mir's dock.

Chiang Gi said, "If they are after us, they will find a watery grave. Long ago in the great days of the Rajah, criminals were executed here by secretly rowing them into this channel and drowning them. They say there were over a hundred, one year. The bones may still be in the mud."

Durell looked back at the pursuing launch. It was closing fast. The river narrowed, with branches overhung and interlaced high above. It was like entering a hot, humid tunnel. Insects whined, bit, and stung. The roar of the motorboat's engine was quite loud now. Chiang turned his pole abruptly and leaned into it. The boat spun on a dime and shot off in a new direction. Mud scraped the bottom, jolting Durell's spine. The little craft heeled far over as the old man put his powerful shoulder to the oar. Again they bumped bottom. A dead tree glimmered briefly ahead. Durell took out his gun.

"Can they follow?"

"They can try."

He counted three men in the launch. It was that close, now. He wasn't sure if Merrydale's face was among the pale, anonymous blobs behind the windshield. The engine was pounding, and the bow-wave made a creamy arc against the dark night. Durell ducked as vines scraped overhead. The channel was very narrow. Chiang Gi began to breathe hard.

"Give me the pole," Durell said.

"I am all right."

"You are seventy years old. Tell me how to go, that's all."

The launch swept past the narrow channel into which they had darted. The sound of its engine echoed away. Durell poled harder, and Chiang Gi sat in the prow, indicating with his left hand for a turn, then waving straight on.

"Can they cut us off?"

"Perhaps, *tuan.*"

"Can we use your outboard?"

"It is very shallow here."

Durell pushed the pole harder into the mud. The channel twisted right, left, and divided among low-growing mangrove islets. Now and then the jungle thinned, and the moonlight shone down, letting him see more clearly. He thought he could hear the sound of the surf somewhere to the north and to the left. The moon swung as the channel turned, came around to their back, then vanished under lacy branches overhead. He saw the twinkling of pale orchids opening for the night. A monkey chattered at them briefly. A bird's wings flashed. He remembered his boyhood in the Louisiana bayou country at Bayou Peche Rouge and did not feel completely lost.

"How much farther, Chiang?"

"Now. To the left."

He shoved the pole into the bank and swung the prow around with a purling of water. A drooping branch slapped his chest. An insect bored into the nape of his neck. Water opened before them, and at the same moment light flickered through the jungle, bright shafts that swung from side to side stabbing through the black trees. Durell braked the boat with the pole, aware of sweat soaking his shirt and back. Chiang Gi held up a hand with fingers spread wide.

"They beat us here. They are waiting."

"I see."

"Motor is off."

"Yes."

The Malay felt around on the bottom of the boat and came up with a long, wickedly curved knife and laid it across his bare knees as he crouched in the prow. His head was bent, as if in thought. Durell debated their chances. There was no hope of reaching the open channel to Pasangara harbor, but there might be a way into the klongs that made a network of waterways through the city. There was a dim glow to the north and east that marked the town. He judged it to be three, perhaps four miles off. Meanwhile, the launch waited. It was invisible except for the probing stabs of light that marked it, the light coming through the branches like the flexing legs of a giant insect stalking in the trees.

He did not know why Paul Merrydale had come after him like this. It might be petty anger because of the shotgun, but he did not think so. A psychosis of pride and frustration might have impelled the man to start out, but this was too careful, too determined, almost professional. He stood up and poled the boat slowly forward along the narrow channel. The wider waterway opened ahead. He saw a gleam of metal reflected from the launch's chrome trim.

On the other hand, it could just be part of the racial madness that had seized the province, with men running amok, slashing and burning.

Either way, you could be just as dead.

It was safe to assume there were arms aboard the launch, perhaps heavy hunting rifles. The shotgun had been bad enough; it would be reloaded now.

The others had made one error, however. Their inboard engine was cut, and they should have left it idling, regardless of the sound, since they were confident enough to give away their position with the spotlight. He turned and considered the shiny new outboard that was Chiang Gi's pride. They hadn't used it yet. He spoke to Chiang in a whisper, and the old man grinned and made a whipping gesture with his hand across his naked chest. They would have to risk it.

He poled cautiously almost to the exit of the tiny canal, keeping themselves hidden behind the mangroves. The spotlight wavered up and down, scanning the tree-tops. He thought he heard voices in Malay, but then a parrot squawked in the vines, and he wasn't sure. You calculate the percentages and then make your try, he thought. Chiang whispered the distances to him, knowing the waterways intimately, and Durell thought about it and saw no way out short of returning the way they had come. But soon the nameless men in the launch would grow impatient and edge into the mangroves, too. Time was running out. If they retreated now, they might be cut off again at the other end. It all depended on the outboard.

The men in the launch were not sure they had arrived yet. Durell looked up at the moon. It was in its third phase and rising now so that its orb was above the trees. He wished there were clouds, but you can't have everything, he thought.

He pulled the lanyard on the outboard engine.

Either it started immediately, or it didn't. If it coughed and died, they would have given themselves away.

The outboard sprang into roaring life that racketed through the jungle. Durell slammed the throttle full over and pointed the bow into the larger waterway. It was a matter of timing. He saw that the width of this arm of the Pasangara river was almost a fifth of a mile across, and there was the glimmer of surf on a shoal far to the right where the sea began. Chiang Gi remained in the prow, his long parang gripped in his hand. The launch was to their left. There was a glimpse of startled faces, a shout, an order. The spotlight swung wildly, stabbing after them, shot overhead, then wavered out across the river. There was stumbling movement in the launch as someone stabbed for the starting button of their engine.

Chiang Gi pointed to starboard, and Durell slammed

the boat that way. They were well out on the river's surface before the launch's engine coughed and roared. From
here Durell glimpsed the riding lights of the tanker out in
the harbor and a blinking navigation beacon atop the
government building. There was a clump of fishing boats
farther downstream near the shoal, but that was much too
far away to reach.

"Straight ahead," Chiang Gi said.

They were halfway across the river before the launch
could swing after them. Its engine made a deep-throated,
implacable roar. There was no hope of outrunning it.

"Left, now," the Malay said quietly.

Durell swung the bow a little, saw Chiang wave for
more, and the little boat heeled sharply, took a long wave
of river water, heeled some more, and then slowly righted.
The spotlight swept over them, came back, held them in
a blinding glare.

There was a sudden series of bumping waves, a large
shoal ripple, and then a wall of blackness looming ahead.
The jungle bank still seemed far away. The launch closed
fast. Durell wondered if they would risk shooting and
decided they could do so, considering the riots in the city.
He felt like a fly pinned to the wall. The open boat shuddered, and the outboard kicked up automatically as the
screw hit bottom. They lost way immediately, drifted, and
he slammed the motor back to vertical. It bit into deeper
water and they surged on. It was all painfully slow. The
launch was close behind them now. He heard a shout,
and then the spotlight slewed off them, canting far to the
left and upward. The pounding of its motor became a
scream of agony as the launch hit the shoal they had just
crossed.

Chiang Gi laughed. "Scratch one," he said.

Durell turned their boat to the right again, then straight
ahead, taking advantage of the confusion aboard the
launch. For a moment, the spotlight had lost them. He
thought he heard a rifle shot, but the bullet came nowhere
near.

"In there," Chiang Gi said. "Right ahead."

Durell could see very little, but there was no time to recover his night vision after the blinding glare of the spotlight. He heard the rifle crash again, and this time a small plume of spray marked where the bullet hit the river's surface, ten feet to starboard. A wall of dark growth rushed at them, grew enormously taller and wider. It seemed certain they would smash into the river bank. Chiang Gi crouched forward, nodded, and they roared into a slot of water between tall trees, dangling vines, and mud banks. Their wake made a splashing wash behind them.

Durell eased back on the throttle.

There were no more shots. The river and the stranded launch were cut off from view.

"From here," Chiang said quietly, "we go straight into the city's canals. Take the first klong to the right, and you will be back at your hotel, *tuan.*"

"And you?"

"It is my birthday," the old man said quietly. "My family waits for me to celebrate."

6

THE Kuan Diop Hotel stood on the river bank next to a small park and boulevard that ran downstream toward the resplendent Government Square. The rioting and fire-bombing had come close to the old hotel but hadn't touched the immediate vicinity. The hotel had been built in Victorian splendor by an enterprising Welshman who had once dreamed of tourists and expansionism. The tourists rarely came, and the promise of rubber and tea in the mountains of the province never materialized. There was another hotel of American style, a sprawling concrete and glass cube on the waterfront near the Chungsu slums, which had been considered colorful by the Madison Avenue executives of the chain. This one was used by diplomats, a few daring tourists, and the local businessmen from the capital. It was mostly empty and echoing, its glitter attracting no one. The Kuan Diop, on the other hand, smaller and cozier, if shabby, was always reasonably full.

Durell's room, procured for him by the consul, faced the river. A stern-wheeler, out of the '90s, was tied up at the dock just beyond the strip of green park. There was a smell of cooking in the seedy corridors, a murmur of radios and conversation behind closed doors. The bar was crowded with Europeans discussing the race riots, red-faced men who drank their gin straight and sweated under the old-fashioned, revolving wooden fans in the high ceiling. Above the bar was a portrait of the first White Rajah of Pasangara, resplendent in white turban and peacock feathers and jeweled pendants. Long ago someone had defaced the portrait by making a scratch across the surface, and it had been poorly repaired. Chinese businessmen huddled by themselves in one corner of the bar and whispered to each other of their losses from firebombing that day and discussed the possibility of insurance from their tong brotherhoods.

Two men were waiting for him in his room.

There was a wide veranda that ran the length of the scrollwork facade of the Kuan Diop, and Durell's windows opened on this with two Bombay chairs aligned to face the park and the dock below. Durell had left the French doors closed and the door locked, but that would not be a problem for these two.

They had helped themselves to his liquor and made themselves comfortable. They got up casually and easily, at home in their own province, sure of themselves and their power. "Mr. Durell?"

He waved a hand. "Help yourself, Colonel."

"Thank you. We have. We apologize for the intrusion."

"Not at all," Durell said blandly.

"We haven't met, but you know me?"

"Everyone in Pasangara knows Colonel Thu Tileong."

"This is my lieutenant, Lieutenant Parepa."

"I am honored."

They were tough and brown and very natty in their khakis, Sam Brownes, and holstered pistols. Very Americanized. Their round faces smiled as impassively as the Buddha's on the temple grounds down the boulevard. The black eyes regarded him blankly. Colonel Tileong was small and slim with a thin moustache apparently grown with difficulty. He didn't feel the heat at all. There was a small scar running from a corner of his mouth down the side of his chin, but it was not unpleasant.

His lieutenant was another matter. Sometimes the Malays grow big, and Parepa was a giant for a Malay, almost Durell's height, and although he tried, Parepa could not put on the veneer of worldly sophistication enjoyed by his superior. Parepa was a murderer. It showed in his broad, harsh face and the downward curve of his mouth and in the way he regarded Durell.

"You left your door unlocked, Mr. Durell. Very careless in these restless times."

"Yes, the times are restless. How many Chinese have been killed so far?"

"Thirty-seven," Parepa said at once.

"And Malays?"

Colonel Tileong intercepted the question. "We did not come here to discuss the disturbances with you, although we would, of course, value your opinion since your own country has seen much racial tension, too. It is all very regrettable—"

"Why are you here, then?"

"Martial law has been declared," said the colonel, "and a curfew as well."

"I see."

"You have violated the curfew. No Europeans are permitted beyond the city boundaries for the next forty-eight hours. You did not know that, of course. However, we are forced, regrettably, to ask you to confine yourself to the hotel grounds until further notice. It is for your own protection, naturally. Tempers are running high, and you might be mistaken by a mob and become an unhappy victim of our misfortune."

"Am I under arrest?" Durell asked.

"Of course not."

"I would like to go to the consulate."

"Ah, yes. Your credentials have been examined by our security people, and there are some questions we have—purely routine, naturally—but nevertheless, you know how bureaucrats love paper work." Colonel Tileong smiled. His hands moved very slightly. Lieutenant Parepa scowled, as if impatient with the courtesies. "Could you be at my office by nine o'clock tomorrow morning?"

"I thought you had just confined me to the hotel."

"Yes, but we will send a car for you. Agreeable?"

"I'm happy to cooperate."

"Ah, one other thing," Colonel Tileong said. "Your gun. Was it declared at customs?"

"What gun?" Durell asked.

"Come, come, Mr. Durell. We *know* who you are. We *know* your position vis à vis Mr. George Hammond. We are surprised, not flattered, that Pasangara merits your attention. We manage our own affairs now. The gun will be returned to you when you leave us."

"All right." Durell took his .38 S & W and handed it to Tileong, who passed it negligently back to Parepa, whose huge paw swallowed it like the mouth of a boa constrictor. "Will I get it back?"

"These are troubled times. The matter will be decided officially. And, ah, one other thing." Colonel Tileong smiled again. Durell preferred him not to. "About the Merrydales, you see. They hold a most, ah, anomalous position here in Pasangara. Descendents of buccaneer royalty, in a sense. There is no harm in them these days; we rather enjoy their presence with us as a reminder of exploitation, a goad to make us preserve our national independence and rights."

"Museum pieces?" Durell asked.

"In a sense. You found Pala Mir well?"

"Yes." He saw no point in denying his visit. It was obvious that Tileong knew all about it, which, in turn, meant that the leak he had suspected at the consulate was much too big for any lad to stop with a finger in the dike.

"What was your business with Pala Mir?"

"A courtesy call."

"Come, come, Mr. Durell."

Durell responded, "If I am under arrest, then take me into custody. If you want to question me, do it officially. If I'm to be interrogated, let's go down to your barracks."

"We are trying to be decent about this, sir."

"Then stop swiping my liquor, breaking into my hotel room, and putting the finger on me. I'm here as second legal secretary to the American consul, Mr. David Condon, and if you wish to declare me persona non grata, do so. Otherwise, I'll have to report harassment by the local authorities."

"You could not report it now," Tileong said. "The cables and phone wires are all down, thanks to the mob violence. We expect the power to go shortly, which will disable all but battery-powered radios."

"You expect this?"

"It is difficult to contain this madness."

"Can't you protect your own power plant?"

"Ah, we have only so many men. We will do our best." Tileong stood up. He was a very small, very dapper man.

Durell said, "I think I prefer to have my gun back, if things are that bad."

"You are not very cooperative, sir."

"I'm sorry I'm not." Durell went across to the center of his room beyond the big bed with its mosquito netting and picked up the telephone on the bamboo table against the wall. Under the telephone was an outdated but still effective J-5 mike and transmitter, a tiny black disc adhered to the plastic. Durell thumbed it off and tossed it through the open French windows over the edge of the balcony. "Yours, Colonel?"

Both military men had been startled by his move. "That was government property—" Tileong began.

His lieutenant was more direct. Parepa had his gun out of its shiny holster, and as Durell turned, the lieutenant slashed at his head with the butt. Durell fell sidewise, aware of pain near the right temple, worried about his right eye, but looking for a chance to knee the big man in the groin. He didn't get it. Parepa was quick for his size, and his fist exploded in Durell's belly. As Durell came forward, Parepa chopped at his neck and drove him flat, face down, on the bed. It would have been easy for Durell to use his heel and hook the big man where it hurt and then come up and smash in Parepa's face, but he lay still, exaggerating his pain, and waited. Parepa seemed satisfied. There was a quick exchange in Malay, and Tileong came over and shook Durell's shoulder.

"Are you all right, Mr. Durell?"

"Never better."

"The floors are slippery. The servants are very zealous with the wax."

"Yes, you are correct."

"I will expect you at my office by nine o'clock tomorrow morning. As I said, one of my cars will pick you up."

"Your hospitality is overwhelming."

Dimly over the night-bound city came the sound of a rolling, thunderous explosion. The windows rattled and the walls of the hotel shook. Plaster came down from the ceiling in small white puffs. The overhead fan stopped working, there was a flickering of the lights, and then they went out.

"Your power plant," said Durell.

In the darkness Tileong's smile could be felt, if not seen. "Ah, yes."

7

SERVANTS in white wraparound skirts came with oil lanterns, chattering softly to themselves. Durell bathed the cut on his head and sent down for some plastic tape. He took one of the lamps into the huge bathroom and considered his right eye in the speckled mirror. Not too bad. He spent twenty minutes going over his room, following the IPS formula, but nothing had been disturbed. Parepa was an amateur. There was nothing he could do about the French doors and the veranda, since any plastic credit card could slip the latch, but he locked the doors, balanced a broken match on top of one, and drew the thin, cotton curtains, arranging the folds from right to left where they rested on the polished teak floor.

There was no need for power in the Chungsu area of the city. Several fires had started there among the defensive Chinese, and the red glow lit up the tropical night over the town. Dimly, he heard fire sirens, the clang of antiquated equipment, and a volley of shots from somewhere else in the city.

The hotel was calm. The clients almost seemed to enjoy the siege. They felt safe, as if it were a picnic. Colonel Tileong had left a company of soldiers bivouacked in the park and the boulevard. Nobody could get in. But no one could get out, either.

By ten o'clock he was ready. He opened the corridor door and saw a young Malay soldier seated in a wicker chair at the end of the hall, a rifle across his knees. Durell went down the wide stairway to the lobby, and the soldier got up and followed him but then seated himself when

Durell went into the bar. The candles and oil lamps that lit up the hotel made deep shadows in the corners and behind the tall columns that supported the high ceiling. There were English, Dutch, French, and Japanese at the bar and at the tables. The Chinese businessmen and shop-keepers had quietly gone away.

Durell had a bourbon and soda and returned to his room. The young soldier followed. In his room he stripped, showered, and changed to a dark business suit he had worn in Taiwan. His luggage had been rifled, but there was nothing overt there that could be pinned on him by the local security people. He went out on the wide veranda that faced the river. A soldier stood at each end, and they turned alertly when he appeared. Smoking a cigarette, he looked down at the river boat and remembered the old *Trois Belles,* the Mississippi side-wheeler on which he had been raised by his Grandpa Jonathan.

The fires still raged in Chungsu.

He yawned elaborately, then turned back to his room to use the telephone. The switchboard was still working. He asked for the consulate. After a time, he was answered by Condon himself. The consul was angry.

"See here, Durell, it seems that you caused some sort of disturbance tonight. There's been a complaint lodged against you by Colonel Tileong."

"And I have a complaint against him. I want to see you, Condon."

"Yes, yes, so I imagine. The Merrydales—"

"Is George Hammond there?"

"No."

"Where is he?"

"I haven't the foggiest idea. What difference does that make?"

"I must see Hammond at once. Send around a consulate car, will you? I'm boxed in here."

"There's a curfew, my dear fellow—"

"You can claim diplomatic immunity," said Durell.

"I'd rather not. See here, I don't know what you are up to or why you're in Pasangara at all, but I've run a tight and tidy ship here, and I'm on good terms with the local authorities, planning to enlarge the Information Library—"

"You'll have to build a new one. It was burned down today, remember? Does George Hammond have a regular driver?"

"Yes, but—"

"Sleeps in the consulate?"

"Yes, but see here—"

"Send him. Fifteen minutes."

Condon was silent, then said quietly, "All right. But I really can't have you—"

Durell hung up.

He returned to the lobby, followed by the soldier as before, and stepped out of the front doors of the Kuan Diop. There was a curving driveway, palm trees, oleanders, neatly trimmed flower beds, and two stone Malay tigers on high pedestals. The boulevard was empty except for small groups of soldiers and an armored car. When Durell went down the steps, the young militiaman tapped his shoulder, said something in Malay, smiled, and shook his head, pointing back to the hotel doors.

Durell nodded, returned the smile, pointed at the car lights swinging up the drive from the wide avenue, then moved lightly down the steps. He was a tall man, heavily muscled in the shoulders, with thick black hair touched with gray at the temples. Condon surely knew he was a field chief of operations for K Section of the Central Intelligence Agency. The consul must have thought better of his objections.

The car was a big Cadillac with American flags in small chrome standards beside the headlights. It slid smoothly to a halt beside Durell. The door swung open, and he got in before the young Malay soldier could run halfway down the steps. The soldier shouted something, but the Cadillac was moving before Durell slammed the door shut. He heard more yelling, and some other troopers dropped the rice they were cooking over small fires on the lawn and began running to the gates. They were too late. Durell looked back and saw one of them pick up the telephone at the hotel door, but he decided that didn't matter.

"Where to, Mr. Durell?" asked the driver.

"Do you know Chiang Gi?"

"He is my grandfather, sir."

"I'd hoped so. Where is Mr. Hammond?"

"With his fiancée, I think."

"In Chungsu?"

"Yes, sir."

"Let's go there."

"It's a bad night for that, sir."

"Step on it."

A siren wailed before they had gone more than five blocks from the hotel. The city was blacked out, but the moon was bright and the fires in the Chinese section added a red glow to the tropical sky. There was some rubble in the streets, torn banners, bricks, and stones. A barricade had been built at one intersection, but it had been overturned and was not manned. Several dark clumps of shadow lay in the gutters under the palm trees, bodies that no one had claimed or bothered to pick up yet. Circling the barrier, the driver was quick and efficient, nicking, however, one timber with a clatter that sent it tumbling across the street.

Headlights flickered behind them. The siren wailed a little louder.

The curfew was effective here. Not a living soul was on the streets. The houses were all dark, the shops shuttered and blank.

The streets became narrow and more twisting as they entered the native quarter. The headlights behind them flickered, vanished, and came on again.

Durell had studied a map of Pasangara's streets when he had first arrived. He leaned forward and touched the driver's shoulder.

"Stop here and let me out. Then keep going as fast as you can for the consulate."

"But you said you wanted to see Mr. Hammond—"

"I'll find him."

"Sir, the streets are dangerous tonight—"

"Stop the car."

Ten seconds later he stood in a shadowed doorway and watched the taillights of the Cadillac vanish down an alley. He stood still. There was a roar from the pursuing car as it rocketed after the Cadillac. Durell saw four troopers with rifles at rest and a driver, their headlights glaring as they screeched around the corner and vanished from sight.

He slowly became aware of the empty silence all around him.

There were papers strewn about, and a tin can glinted in the narrow street. There was a smell of cooking in the air and a smell of something charred and burned, too. An overturned noodle stand lay on the sidewalk. Chinese lanterns had been torn and shredded by an angry mob that had passed this way. Some of the Chinese signs of the shops had been left to litter the sidewalk. He heard a cat mewl, then a dog bark. He heard nothing human, anywhere.

Durell had been with K Section for more years than he cared to remember. His contract was due for its annual renewal in two weeks, and he knew that short of death or serious injury, his file would remain open. General McFee, that small, anonymous gray man who ran K Section, would never let him out, any more than George Hammond had been permitted a peaceful day for the rest of his life. There were dossiers on Durell at No. 2 Dzherzinsky Square in Moscow, where the reconstituted MVD had its headquarters. The Russian Ministerstvo Vnuternikh Dyel—the secret police known as the MVD—would be happy to close the book on him. So, too, would Peking's dreaded Black House.

He began walking east toward the waterfront. It was like walking through a city of the dead.

Long ago you were a boy growing up in the Cajun bayou country of Louisiana with old Grandpa Jonathan, living aboard the hulk of the *Trois Belles*. The old man had been the last of the Mississippi riverboat gamblers, and from his quiet and patient teaching you learned to hunt bigger game than birds and foxes in the moss-draped lagoons and waterways of the delta parishes.

Later there had been Yale, a New England polish, a law degree, and K Section. You were in the silent, underground war before you knew it, driven by a dedication you sometimes denied and a love for freedom and dignity that sounded archaic on today's campuses. You never talked about it. You just did your job. You worked and trained at mnemonic patterns, weaponry, analysis and synthesis, and program patterns for situation problems that other men had paid with their lives to perfect.

Light gleamed ahead. It was one of the narrow klongs that intersected the old slum section of the city near the waterfront. He saw moonlight on the water. There was a gleam of glass from a lantern on one of the nested sampans tied up near the bridge. A child cried but was quickly hushed. It was the first human sound he had heard since he had taken to foot.

He was aware of his vulnerability. He could be shot as a looter, or on any pretext, with the tightly clamped curfew now in effect throughout the city. Apologies would be sent to Washington, but no excuses tendered. Keeping to the shadows, he drifted silently toward the bridge.

At the corner there was a wider street, an embankment on the canal that twisted in from the river. He turned left along a line of shops that were scarred with broken windows, hastily repaired with boarding. The sampans at the bridge were like a huddle of sheep, waiting for circling wolves. He thought he saw a man's head pop up briefly, turn and watch him, and then duck out of sight again. Their fear was greater than his, he reflected.

Beyond the bridge were more shops, and walking past a Chinese herbalist's, he glanced at the red and gold sign and the dragon painted over the door, then went on. At the corner, satisfied, he circled back behind the huddled, shanty-type tenements, found the alley Hammond had once described, and walked into its darkness with care.

No one was waiting for him. The back door was not locked. He smelled spices, ground roots, and pepper. He stepped inside. The darkness was absolute except for a glimmer of moonlight from an upper window that fingered the stairway. He went up the steps in silence.

The apartment was furnished with a huge Chinese bed, some porcelains that might or might not have been genuine, a straw rug, bamboo jalousies. Birds or mice rustled on the attic beams overhead. There was a small kitchen, a table and four chairs, a Japanese tatami mat beside the bed, a stained enameled coffeepot on the two-burner stove. A smell of stale cigar smoke tainted the air. A fine ivory Mah-Jongg set lay scattered in flowered tiles on a low table, and on the walls were Arabian brass plates and an old musket. In one corner was a small stone Buddha with incense pots under his smiling, serene countenance.

Durell looked in the tiny bath, saw a shaving brush with dried lather on it and a razor glinting in the moonlight that came through the window. He stood at the window for a few minutes, looking down at the klong and the nearby bridge. If you watched for birds long enough and silently enough, they thought you were a tree or a bush or a shadow and went about their normal activities.

But nothing was normal about this night in Pasangara.

He felt the tension as surely as one senses the electricity in the air before a thunderstorm.

The night was hot and windless. The apartment above the Chinese apothecary's shop was stifling. Durell moved prudently to save his energy. He looked over the bed, found an Mk. 4 recorder bugged to the mattress, and was not amused. There was another recorder in the bathroom, fitted over the cabinet. He did not detach either mechanism, although he was aware that the sounds he had made in entering, however slight and careful, had activated the batteries, and the little spools were silently whirling, recording all his movements.

There was a large wardrobe of ornate, carved mahogany, a modern piece perhaps from Hong Kong, with circular *yin* and *yang* symbols on each of the two doors. He did not touch it for a moment but used his pencil flash to study the carvings and the big brass key that hung at an obtuse angle in the simple lock. It was pointed at an angle equivalent to forty degrees on a compass rose. Two wires were connected to the hinges, very thin and filmy stuff. He traced them to the back and removed them from the terminals of what would be a very loud and noisy alarm. Then he turned the key upright, due north and south, turned it to the left twice, and the wardrobe opened.

There was only clothing inside—Chinese costumes, black trousers, jackets, a beautifully embroidered coat with mother-of-pearl and gold-braid dragons on the back. Most of the clothing was a woman's. The scent was light, delicate, exotic. There were also several very short, filmy nylon nighties, a garter belt, and a pair of high-heeled straw pumps, sitting cozily beside a man's worn leather bedroom slippers. With the pencil flash Durell studied the interior walls and dimensions and decided there were no hidden compartments. Then he carefully closed the wardrobe, replaced the key at the 40° angle, hooked up the alarm wires again, and turned to the big, red-lacquered Chinese chest against the opposite wall.

That had to be it.

There were double doors and the outside panels were easy enough. As he opened them, however, moving very slowly and resting on his haunches before the cabinet, he heard the faintest click, then a dim whirring, another click, and then silence. He stood up at once and backed away, dousing his light and wiped his hands on a handkerchief, and went back to the window.

The alley and the klong beyond were silent and black under the big moon. The sky over Chungsu, a mile away, still glowed red, but he no longer heard any sirens. Nothing moved down there except a cat that lazily crossed the alley and the embankment and jumped aboard one of the moored sampans near the bridge.

He returned to the cabinet and considered the two inner doors. These were also lacquered, with applied mold-ings in an ornate Chinese design. He ran his fingers over the pattern and found the two strips that were raised frac-tionally above the others. They connected to the hinges. Durell began to sweat a little. It was not going to be as easy as the wardrobe.

He wondered how much time he had.

It would be a JP-6 device, he decided, with enough plastic explosive behind the inner doors to blow his stom-ach against the opposite wall. He did not hesitate. He pressed both thumbs against the ends of the raised embel-lishments on the twin panels, exerted pressure, and twisted simultaneously, the right thumb going counterclockwise, the left rotating to the right. Nothing happened. He drew a deep breath and tried again, using more force this time. There was a second click-whir-click sequence. The pencil flash, on the floor at his right knee, was no help now since he had to use both hands. He pushed hard, and the panel suddenly released itself, coming down forward across his thighs as he knelt before the cabinet.

He was in.

8

ONE side of the interior had shelves stocked with file folders on the lower level and an aerial Epsilon-V camera for infrared exposures at 10,000 feet altitude above sea level. Durell opened the camera and saw it was empty, but there were cannisters of film that were still sealed and unexposed, and he left them all where they had been positioned. He riffled through the file folders, found a tab marked "Thrasher: BETA 77/c," and put it on the floor beside him.

On a second shelf were folded maps, and he took these out, spread one, and saw three plotted courses, heading from 27° to about 208° south, on an old AAF Aeronautical Chart Numbered 859 that showed the coast of Malaya with the Goening Benom mountain in Negri Sembilan province outlined with an angry-red grease pencil. The Pasangara River twisted by devious routes toward the mountain from the marshy, jungled shore of the delta. The chart was on a scale of 1:1,000,000 marked 000-E 10200 / 400Nx600 and dated AIC Nov. 1949. The equipment was outdated.

The middle shelf held a tape recorder, an audioscreening device, and a tiny oscilloscope screen. There was a spool of tape on the recorder, and Durell turned the volume down to its lowest pitch before snapping it on. The recorder hummed and the spools turned. He heard nothing. He turned the volume up higher, and presently he heard a faraway sound, a whisper, a growing roar, a screaming that made him quickly turn it down again. There was a long blank, hissing silence, and then the sounds were repeated two more times.

Thrasher engines.

The spool turned and turned for several moments, and then there were pilots' voices:

"Running low, Theta Hammer Five."

"No sweat."

"How much longer?"

"Four minutes, thirty seconds."

"I'll have to ditch, Theta Hammer."

"Hang on, old buddy."

The voices were mixed—a Midwestern nasal tone, an Alabama drawl, a Yankee twang.

"Theta Hammer Seven, for Christ's sake, where are we?"

"Don't worry."

"Overdue by forty-nine minutes. Jesus, the old man will skin us."

"We're expected, I told you."

"Listen, I—"

"Maintain radio silence, please."

"I don't give a damn what you say, old buddy, I'm turnin' back. My daddy tol' me never to trust to no strangers—"

"Shut up, redneck."

Durell turned to the audioscreening mechanism and the oscilloscope. It was an electronic device used to amplify and select any constant in mixtures of sound, such as traffic, group conversation, or machinery. It could pick out in traffic the characteristic clicking of tappets on one single vehicle out of dozens; in conversation, a single voice in a group debate; in machinery, a particular motor out of a factory floor full of operating hardware. The oscilloscope blinked on with a green glow when he threw the switch; then it showed a series of undulating, widely varying lines. He pushed a second button and the lines flattened, became constant as they were supposed to.

"No sweat. Four minutes, thirty seconds."

And: "Don't worry. We're expected, I told you. Maintain radio silence."

There had been three sequences of Thrasher jets, three pilots' exchanges, and in all of them, one engine and one voice were the only constant.

Durell snapped off everything, picked up his pencil flash, and considered the dossier file marked "Thrasher: BETA 77/c." There were two sheets of flimsies typed on what looked like a West German Olympia with Congressional type:

```
            PANDA PAS/1/1 SOLO HUNGER
                 CLASS. AA/1/AA

Coordinates follow:
  11/9/69@ 7°-N 104° YIELD 6° 103.66°E Kuantan
6440 118.1mc Zed Gamma Freddie 2. Alt. 2500 est.
lowering.
  11/22/69@ 7.4°N 103.9E Do above Alt. 4700 est.
lowering.
```

12/19/69@ 7.1°N 103.9°E CS Zed Gamma Freddie
———. .——. ..—. Visib. Tanjong Gelang Fl.7 sec.
40 lowering fm. 2000 alt. est.

URGENT PANDA PAS / ONE: EPSILON-V and Screen
5 Mk.7. Deliver by Williams.

XX CLASS 2: Monitor since 12/19/69 NEG. Monitor
all flights PANDA PAS/1 Neg. Surveillance 24 hrs.
neg. DRONE JUDAS 1 course 0°45'E dates 12/6—12/18—
12/22—12/30—1/4—1/7 ALL NEG.

On the second typewritten sheet of onionskin was a
report:

PANDA/PAS 2/SOLO HUNGER ALPHA
Classification: AA/11/AA MAKE IT AA/1—1/AA
Subject: Judas 12, THRASHER 3.
Auth: K sec 5 MALAY SUEZ/McF. ltr 2/J
Funds: 22, General.
File: 77-K Sec. 556/ALPHA 2.
Summary:
In view of local difficulties, request urgent
Lotus plane with Epsilon-V to scan areas and
coordinates given last 12/20/ and chute Eps. to
Coordinate 22xPhillipsx4. Will pick up. If Lotus
denied, must go overland, estimated probability
success less than 5%. No local recognition, no
official complaints. Request urgent dossier
Premier Kuang, suggest replacement David Condon.
Any info Merrydales, hist. and contemp. bg.,
highly desirable. Could use field agent under K
Control.
The vanishment of Thrashers definitely ident.
this area above described dates. Three only. No
reports other locates. Reported to Adm. Pentemore,
Navy Dpt. 4, in triplicate, as to Gen. D. McF.
Will continue invest.
Repeat data Merrydales send soonest.

Durell returned the typewritten sheets to the folder and put the folder back with the others in the Chinese cabinet. He smelled faint incense in the air, and somewhere, not too far off, a dim gong sounded in one of the alleys. It was the first human-made sound he had heard since entering the apartment. He straightened, dried his hands again, and considered the four drawers in the opposite side of the cabinet.

In the third drawer down from the top, he found four handguns. He chose a Walther P-38 and a box of cartridges for it, loaded it, and went to the window. The alley and the canal were silent and deserted. From far away he thought he heard a cry, but it could have been a dog, a bird, or a cat. Or it could have come from a man's agonized throat or from a woman's pleading mouth. He looked up at the moon through the window and was surprised at how much time had gone by.

The Walther P-38 felt heavy and solid. He closed the cabinet with as much care as he had used when opening it and then went to the big Chinese platform bed where he stretched out with the gun in his hand so that he could watch the door to the apartment.

He waited for someone to come up the stairs.

9

THE footsteps ascended as lightly as a zephyr, almost taking him by surprise. The moon now cast its shadowy light directly on the doorway, leaving Durell in darkness on the bed. He did not move. The door opened and closed silently. The air was still and hot. The shadows in the room were very black or silvered by the moonlight. He heard breathing, a quick and shallow sound, as if the person had been running. He held the gun ready.

It was a girl. She stepped forward lightly, her head high with a sense of pride and dignity in the way she cocked it. She looked something like a fawn investigating an unfamiliar woodland, almost on tiptoe, ready for instant flight.

She did not see Durell in the shadows that hid the bed.

When she crossed to the wardrobe chest, he saw that she was Chinese.

She behaved at home here. Her black hair caught the moonbeams and shone with glossy life. It was cut in a straight line across her forehead, and her round face was startlingly beautiful, innocent, and young. Her breasts were more fully developed than those of the average Chinese girl; her legs were long, slender, and lithe. She smiled to herself and detached the alarm wire with familiarity from the wardrobe and hummed to herself as she opened the doors.

Durell lay still, watching, the gun ready. She seemed harmless; but in this business, you never knew.

With a swift hissing sound, she undid the zipper of her dark, embroidered dress that was like a mini-*chamesong*, slit high up on the thigh; she stepped out of it gracefully, kicked off her sandals, reached behind her shoulders to undo her brassiere.

Durell did not move.

When she was naked, she moved like a dream of innocence into the tiny bath adjacent to the big room, and he heard the sound of water running in the tub. Somewhere in the town a siren began to wail again. A cock crowed, although it wasn't midnight yet. The girl was a long time in the tub. He couldn't see her, but he heard her splashing and occasionally humming a little Chinese song. Her words were in *pai-hua,* the simple Chinese detached from Mandarin *Kuo-yü.* She seemed very sure of herself and of her presence in this place, and he considered it for a while and started to get out of bed very quietly, then thought better of it and remained where he was.

She came out presently, a towel about her slender body. She dropped the towel on the floor when she returned to the wardrobe and selected one of the thin nylon nighties he had seen hanging there. With her arms raised she looked like a nymph, her smooth young face inexpressibly lovely in the moonlight.

Then she saw him.

It might have been a glimmering reflection on the barrel of his Walther P-38, pointed at her. Or perhaps she saw his eyes in the darkness.

She was very good.

She didn't jump or scream or dart for the door to escape. She didn't move at all. She stood very still, her head turned to face him as he sat on the bed, and he thought that any young girl realizing she had been observed in her intimate privacy would, at least, have cried out. But her face was expressionless, drained of the quiet joy that had been evident before. Her black almond eyes were steady, meeting his. She held her pose for a few long moments, then—

"Who are you?" she whispered.

"A friend of George's."

"George sees no friends here."

"He sees you," Durell suggested.

"I—I'm different. We—we're to be married."

Saying nothing, he continued to sit on the bed, holding the gun. She was aware of it, but she didn't look directly at it or react to it in any overt way. Her self-assurance was a little disturbing.

She said, "I'm Lily Fan. The premier of Pasangara is my father through his second wife."

"His favorite daughter, I'll bet."

"Yes," she said, "I am his favorite."

"Does he approve of you and George?"

"No."

"Do you visit George often here, like this?"

"Yes."

She said it simply, almost with pride, her small chin raised, her almond eyes defiant. Durell got up off the bed, the gun in his hand hanging at his side, and moved out of the black shadows that had hidden him. He stood in the shaft of moonlight shining through the window so she could get a good look at him. He was careful with his movements, as he would have been with a wild woodland animal, not wanting to frighten her into flight. She didn't back up or move away from him. Except for the quick rise and fall of her small round breasts and a certain posture, as if she were on her toes and ready to whirl and run, she seemed calm and sure of herself. Maybe, he thought, that was because she was the daughter of Premier Kuang.

When she saw his face, Lily Fan said, "Oh, you must be Sam Durell."

"Hammond mentioned me, did he?"

"Oh, yes. This morning, he told me about you."

"Did he, really?"

"He said you are an old friend in the same agency with him."

"What agency is that?" Durell asked.

"Oh, George doesn't tell me too much. You don't have to worry about that. He is very careful, even with me."

"I'll bet."

"He *is!*" Her exclamation was defensive. "He is a fine, good, wonderful man, who has been so terribly, terribly hurt in his life so many times, and I love him dearly—"

He interrupted with deliberate brutality. "You're a little young for him, aren't you, Lily?"

"Age makes no difference when one loves the soul as well as the—as well—"

She dropped her glance, and he saw the thick black arcs of her lashes. They formed little fans on her round cheeks, and her face was like a lily, too, and he decided she was aptly named. Her aura of innocence was incredible. Standing as she did in her brief nylon nightdress, her black hair tied up with a ribbon in a bun at the top of her small head, she was an object of every man's desire. She opened her black eyes wide, suddenly.

"George didn't say you were coming tonight."

"No, I suppose he didn't."

"And no one is supposed to know this is his place."

"That's right."

"How did you find it? Are you angry with George? You *sound* angry. You will please point that gun away from me? It makes me so nervous. Please?"

She didn't look nervous at all. She came closer to him at last, and still as if on tiptoe, she looked up at his height, his sun-browned face, his eyes that looked black in the moonlight. She touched his cheek.

"Oh, you are a friend," she whispered.

"I don't think so."

"You will not hurt Lily Fan, will you?"

He was silent.

"Or George? I love George. He is so wonderful—"

"George is a tired old man," Durell said harshly. "And you know too much, Lily."

She was quick, but not quick enough, as she tried for his gun. He held it with a deliberate appearance of looseness in his fingers at his side, and her knowledge of grips and holds would have done credit to the training given to K Section people at the Maryland "Farm." She was small but adept and strong, and she almost threw him off balance with her heel hooked behind his, her chop at his throat, her knee rising to smash into his groin. He avoided the last, countered her chop by catching her wrist, twisting the fragile bones down and outward, and at the same time, he pinned her, all in one movement, around the end of the Chinese platform bed and threw her backward. She landed with a thud, bounced, tried to rise, but he was over her kneeling, his forearm across her throat, applying just enough pressure to warn her that her larynx would be crushed if she resisted.

She lay still, her breathing fast and light, a little smile on her full lips. Her eyes were locked with his in challenge without dismay or apology for her attack.

"You're pretty good, Lily Fan."

"I will have you deported," she said quietly. "My father rules this province. Perhaps I will ask him to throw you into jail. The jail in Pasangara is not a nice place. It would be doing George a favor, since you do not like George, it seems. Please, you are hurting me."

"Then behave."

Kneeling over her on the bed, her nylon nightie up over her waist, he turned his head at a sound and saw George Hammond standing in the doorway.

10

HE looked tall and cadaverous in the moonlight, leaning a little to the left to favor his old injuries. His thick gray hair was unkempt, and his seersucker suit looked as if he had slept in it. His eyes were sunk into deep hollows, gleaming with a feral light as he took in the scene. But he had been in the business too long to jump to premature conclusions. His voice was dry.

"Having fun, Cajun? Get up out of there, Lily."

"Oh, George—it's not—he tried—"

"Be quiet. Stand up, Cajun. I have a gun on you."

"That doesn't surprise me."

"I mean it. You don't belong here."

"I think I do. You didn't give me much in the way of directives on this assignment."

Hammond didn't move from the doorway. His voice was quiet, but there was a tremor in it that revealed the rage that must be storming in him.

"I'm your control in Pasangara, Cajun. You take orders from me. I give you as much data as I think you need, no more, no less, to function properly. What I tell you or do not tell you is always up to my own discretion."

"Yes, and you do your homework, George, although not always according to procedure."

Hammond's gleaming eyes flickered to the girl. She walked quickly into the bathroom and closed the door, as if he had given her a spoken order. "You don't have to worry about Lily Fan."

"I worry about everything in Pasangara."

"Yes, you have good reason to. Colonel Tileong is looking for you. Your usefulness here is at an end, Cajun. I'm already filing a report to that effect. Taiwan is sending a plane down for you tomorrow, at my request, if the airfield is functioning. Dispatches have gone to Kuala Lumpur about you. You're blown sky-high."

"And who talked about me, George?" Durell was quiet but equally angry. "Pala Mir knew me, her brother knew me, I'm the victim of a murder attempt in the jungle, I'm confined to the hotel—and my cover as a legal secretary at the consulate is a joke to everyone in authority here. I've been on many jobs, George, but I've never run into a situation run as carelessly as this. A man could get killed this way."

"That's right," Hammond said gently.

The sound of running water came from the bathroom. Hammond cocked his head, as if listening to the noises made by the Chinese girl there, then shrugged and took his hand out of his pocket. Durell felt a little easier. Everything Hammond had said about being his control was true. He had violated procedures himself by breaking into Hammond's safe house here and invading the files. K controls were always in command. He felt sorry for Hammond because Hammond was trying to do a job here without adequate resources; he was out of touch with new procedures and rusty on his technique, perhaps too old and too tired to be trusted. A cardinal rule was that you took no unnecessary chances first with your assignment, then with your life. On the one hand, you didn't violate upper levels of security on your own initiative. Hammond represented such an upper level. He had every authority to remove Durell from Pasangara. On the other hand, there was Lily Fan.

"Do you trust her?" Durell asked quietly, nodding at the bathroom door.

"Of course. We're going to be married."

"And Premier Kuang approves?"

"Why not?"

"You're older than she. You're not from a fine overseas Chinese family. You have no money except for your salary and K Section funding. How old is Lily Fan? Twenty?"

"Twenty-two."

"And politically aware?"

"*A*political."

"How can you be sure? Young people are concerned about the world in a way that you and I never were at their age. And with overseas Chinese, you can never be certain."

Hammond hesitated. "I've checked her out. She went to the University of Tokyo. And Berkeley in California. Precocious intellectually. And yet—like a child, you know?" He smiled wanly. "Look, Cajun, we have to work together. I admit it looked like hell seeing you with her like that, but let's not argue about it. We have the Thrashers to think about."

"That's why I'm here," Durell said. "But you seem to have other things on your mind."

"You think I'm an old fool?"

"You're almost forty years her senior. If you want her in bed with you, and she's willing—fine. But what's all the talk about marrying her?"

"She wants to marry me."

"How much does she know about you?"

"Nothing," Hammond insisted.

"Can she get into your files?"

"No."

"Has she tried?"

"She exhibits no curiosity about my work. Oh, she knows I'm engaged in some security investigations for the consulate, but that's all. It means nothing to her."

There was a small pause between them, and in it

Durell heard a small murmuring sound from across the city, coming from the waterfront. Evidently Colonel Tileong's curfew was not fully operative. He went to the window and looked down the alley at the sampans tied up at the bridge, but all was dark and silent down there. Behind him, Hammond coughed.

"I'm sorry, Sam, I've said things I didn't really mean. But you can understand, I come in here and see you on the bed with Lily—"

Durell said nothing. There was much between them that would always have to remain unspoken. He felt impatient with himself, precisely because he knew George Hammond's anguish and desperation. Emotion was a dangerous ingredient in this game.

In Taipei when he was briefed by Dickinson McFee, the general had said, "George is your nominal control, of course, but you are on your own in Pasangara, Samuel. Hammond has been in a backwater too long; he's both physically and mentally debilitated. It's too bad, but he's there, and you will have to cope with him, somehow, without bumping him too hard."

"Hammond once taught me a great deal," Durell had said.

"He was one of the best. But he made a mistake—just once."

"How bad is he?"

McFee said quietly, "Don't let him get in your way, but try not to let him know it, just the same. He was a fine man and a good friend."

"Is he safe?"

McFee's answer was short. "No."

Durell listened to more water splashing in the bathroom where Lily Fan still lingered. Hammond sighed and took out one of his long, thin cigars, bit off the end and lit it, the match making a tiny bomb flare of light that temporarily washed out the brilliance of the Malayan moon. His face was all hollows and agonies in the glow of the cigar. When he sat down, he put his left leg straight out before him.

"Did you get into the safe, Cajun?"

"Yes."

"Who briefed you on this place?"

"General McFee."

"I thought nobody knew about it. It wasn't in any of my reports. It's that little pip-squeak Condon. He's snooping, of course. He did a tour of duty in the Navy, and he's ONI, I'm sure. Naturally, Navy Intelligence wants to know about their Thrashers, but they've no idea where the planes went, and they simply alerted Condon to nose around. It's a question of too many agencies proliferating around one job. We hug our secrets to ourselves, and the left hand doesn't know what the right is doing."

"Are you sure about the consul?"

"Oh, yes," Hammond said. "He's the one who has been reading me out. He's from the new school, though. Who can you trust these days? His politics are unreliable, I'd say. No record of open campus radicalism, but he's one of them, eager to build a new world of love-ins and pantheistic rites but wanting to drive there in a shiny little bug of a sports car that Daddy's hard-working cash bought for him. It's only because of his family that he's in the Foreign Service at all. What these long-haired pip-squeaks don't seem to think about is who is going to produce the things mankind needs to survive while they're gamboling about asexually in the meadows?"

"What did Condon do in the Navy?" Durell asked.

Hammond's grin was skeletal. "He was a pilot, old buddy. He never flew Thrashers—they're new—but he could certainly handle one if he had to. Interesting?"

"Could be. We have a Judas among us."

"And then you have our Colonel Tileong," Hammond said. He drew deeply on the cigar and rubbed his left thigh, as if it ached. It probably did. "Tileong was educated in England—a military education. Air Force, too. Checked out in jets, too. He could fly a Thrasher as easily as he handles a rubber hose in that security fort of his.

And he's often absent from town. I've tried to correlate his disappearances from Pasangara with the times the Thrashers were taken but haven't had much luck in that direction yet. Neither good nor bad reports. He's a tough little fellow—fanatically devoted to his country and its freedom."

"Why not?" Durell said. "Did you ever get me a dossier on Paul Merrydale?"

"No chance yet. Kuala Lumpur hasn't answered my inquiry. The lines are down, or maybe they're just closed by Tileong to suit his convenience. Paul is in business here, though; it would seem that he'd be anxious to stay in right with Kuang's premiership and the regime. Especially in view of the old man, the former White Rajah. Paul Merrydale and Condon make a pair, all right. Drinking buddies, they are. Chiang Gi says he heard them talk about flying one night. Paul seemed to be knowledgeable about jets, and I've heard that he did a trick of military service, too, but there's a blank spot in his career. He was gone from Pasangara for two years, something like Pala Mir's society tour of Europe. But Pala Mir blazed a wide trail from the Riviera to Peking, while Paul's two years are still a closed book."

The noise from the waterfront was growing louder and more distinct. It was a mob sound, mindless and dangerous. It seemed to be coming this way.

"Who owns this herbalist's shop?" Durell asked.

Hammond grinned. "It belongs to Chiang Gi's brother. He's off on a visit to other relatives in Hong Kong."

"You lean on Chiang Gi a lot, it seems."

"He's invaluable."

"But many of these overseas Chinese here and in Southeast Asia have families and home ties back on the mainland," said Durell.

"Well, that's true, and no doubt many have a deep loyalty to the motherland and even to the Peking regime, for all we know. But I'd stake my life on Chiang Gi's loyalty to me."

"You may have to," Durell said shortly.

The sound of water in the bath ended abruptly.

Hammond sighed and looked at the closed door.

"Am I a fool, Cajun?" he asked quietly.

"Perhaps."

"I love Lily. I tell you, I love her."

"December and May," Durell said.

"Is that so wrong?"

"It's wrong."

"She's a fine, sweet, wonderful girl."

"She's a child."

"No," Hammond said. "She's a woman."

"You could be her grandfather."

"But I'm not, am I? Do you know what it's been like for me ever since East Germany? For a long time I woke up with nightmares, sweating and shaking all over. I lost my nerve, I admit it. Any man would after getting their special treatment. I used to think I was tough enough to take anything. But I'm not. Neither are you. I hope to God you never find that out about yourself. It's a rotten, miserable, cruel business. Afterward, I wanted out; I wanted to be like everyone else. Don't you ever feel like that, Cajun?"

"Yes. Often."

"But it's too late for you, just as it's too late for me. I thought for a while that our own people were going to kill me. I was just deadwood, a total loss. Oh, I could see it in their eyes. The agency had no further use for me. I was a physical and mental wreck after East Germany, and in the agency's eyes, I was a dangerous one."

"You did fine," Durell said. "You recovered."

Hammond shook his gaunt head. A loop of thick gray hair fell over his eyes, and he brushed it away. His hand was shaking.

"But you know, nobody spoke honestly to me after that. I was given every kind of treatment. The psychiatrists had a field day, debriefing me for over two years. They wiped out part of my memory, part of my life. Maybe it helped; maybe it didn't. I'm not the same as I was; that's all I know. But I want to go back there."

"Where?"

"To where I was before it happened, before they got me in East Germany." He paused. "They just use the same Gestapo techniques, but now it's for the cause of socialism."

"The agency took care of you," Durell said. "They didn't arrange for a phony suicide or an accident or have a doctor stick a needle in you to put you to sleep for good, did they? You were given good jobs."

"Useless jobs," Hammond said bitterly. "Like this one in Pasangara. I was no good as a civilian and no good to the agency." He paused again. "You son of a bitch, are you patronizing me?"

"No. I can see myself in you, George."

"No, you can't. You don't believe it can happen to you. But it will. It always does. To all of us." Hammond's cigar had gone out. He struck another match, and the tiny flare illuminated the deep crevasses in his cadaverous face. His eyes under his heavy brows and bony ridges were dark and inscrutable. "This is my chance to get back into the middle of things, Cajun. Maybe you have orders to supersede me, I don't know. I haven't had any directives about you, but in any case, I'm not going to let you get in my way. I'm on to something about the Thrashers, and I'm going to make it back this time. I have to prove something to myself."

"Or to Lily Fan," Durell said.

"Yes. Maybe. I love her," he said again.

The bathroom door opened and the Chinese girl came out.

She had changed back to her street dress, and in the moonlight that now flooded the room, there was a childlike innocence about her appearance. She had brushed her glossy black hair and renewed the doll-like straight bangs across her forehead. She walked at once to Hammond, who remained in the chair smoking his cigar, and put her hand possessively on his shoulder. "Is it all right, George?"

"No need to worry, Lily. The Cajun understands."

"I had better go home, then."

"I'll take you," Hammond said. His thick brows lifted in irony. "That is, if Durell has no objections."

Durell said, "You may have to wait awhile."

Like a sudden tidal wave of noise and crashing violence, the mob, carrying torches, had crossed the bridge and erupted among the moored sampans there. Durell went to the window and looked down. He thought he heard a girl scream, and there were shouts of men and another scream—and then he saw the girl, running, fleet as a doe, from the bridge and down the alley toward the apothecary's place.

All at once, he knew the girl was heading for him. But she would never make the house. The mob came on like a flood tide, spreading out in long, dark tentacles, no longer composed of individuals but a destructive entity with all its energy aimed on the capture and annihilation of that single, fleet figure of a girl.

Then she turned her head, and for a brief moment, Durell glimpsed her tormented, terrified face, lighted by the red glare of the torches.

It was Pala Mir, running for her life.

11

DURELL went down the back stairs three at a time, came out in the dark little area that was fenced off from the alley, and stepped through the gate. He had his Walther P-38 in his hand. The roar of the angry mob filled the hot, midnight air like the savage pounding of an angry surf. The narrow walkway between the tenements was dark and deserted. He drifted quietly to the left and came to the entrance of the Chinese apothecary's shop. In the glare of the mob's torches, he saw the jars of snake oil, dried toads, and hanging strings of herbs and roots behind the dusty glass. It was only a few steps across the narrow, dusty street to the embankment of the klong. Someone had thrown a torch into one of the sampans, and the straw-plaited cabin had gone up like a bomb, lighting the area at one end of the bridge. There were screams and splashings as the Chinese fishermen dived for safety into the black water.

He couldn't see the girl.

The crowd had been momentarily distracted by the burning sampan and the prospective victims who poured from the little boats around it. There were a few moments of time. He crossed the narrow street quickly and stood in the shadows of a flame tree that grew at a tormented angle over the water.

He called softly. "Pala? Pala Mir?"

But there was no chance that he could be heard above the murderous shouts and screams from the bridge. He searched the rank grass and brush that grew along the edge of the klong. The girl had vanished completely. The mob hadn't gotten her yet. He eased down to the water's edge and saw a ripple on the surface of the canal, and then her hand came up, wet and dripping, and caught his.

"Wait. Stay there," he said.

"Durell? Is it really you?"

"Take it easy."

Her long black hair clung to her face and shoulders. Her dress had been torn, and there was a bad scratch on her left cheek and blood on one hand. Her eyes were wide and blind with terror, her head moved from side to side waiting for the mob to come on. Durell looked back and decided the apothecary's shop was no place to take her now. It had to be kept out of the public eye, at all costs. He knelt by the water's edge.

"Can you swim a little more?"

"I—I don't know. I've been—running so long. I was

going to see my grandfather, and they came out of nowhere. I don't think—they don't know who I am—"

"Here they come again," said Durell quietly.

He slid into the warm, turgid water of the canal beside her. But it was too late. Someone, a tall, half-naked man waving a blood-stained parang gave a shout, spotting them. Racing toward them, the mob roared and surged along the embankment of the klong.

Durell held the girl's hand and dived. Twisting, she went under the surface with him. Weeds and reeds and all sorts of rotting vegetation and trash littered the canal bottom. His clothing bubbled and sucked him backward, but he managed to thrust the gun into his waistband with his free hand and stay underwater, striking out for the opposite bank that was hidden in shadows. Something overhead struck the surface of the water. He thought it was a rock, thrown by one of the mob. He felt Pala Mir's body writhe spasmodically and knew he had to surface to give her air. He held her tighter, let her come up briefly, and in the one moment when they both gulped gratefully and filled their lungs, he heard the single report of a gun and saw the bullet splash the surface of the canal only a few feet from their heads.

But the trajectory was not from the direction of the pursuing crowd.

He dived again, dragging the exhausted girl with him underwater, fighting against the sluggish current that came in from the tidal reach of the river. The girl's arms came frantically around his neck, dragging him down. His shoulder struck something underwater, and he saw it was a heavy stake, driven into the mud bottom as a navigation guide. He came to the surface behind it in its narrow shadow and pulled Pala Mir up with him.

"I can't—" she gasped. "My arm—"

"Hang on. Don't choke me."

For a moment the maddened people had lost them. They had gone on down the embankment past the spot where he had found Pala Mir. From a corner of his eye he thought he saw shadows move in the darkness of the opposite bank. He and Pala Mir had gone only half-way across the klong. There were taller, better houses on the far side, but they were all tightly shuttered against the violence that raged in the city. He looked back again, and at the same moment a second bullet hit the pole that sheltered them and sent splinters flying into the water. The slug screamed over the canal beyond them.

He couldn't see the rifleman beyond the glare of the torches. He thought of George Hammond with Lily Fan in the upper window above the herbalist's shop.

"Come on," he muttered.

Pala Mir's extraordinary eyes shone dully; she was in the last stage of exhaustion. Her mouth was open, and her teeth gleamed between her full lips. He saw that her left arm had been cut and was still bleeding. He spoke to her again, and when she didn't reply but remained clinging to the pole in the canal, he slapped her face lightly. When that had no effect, he kissed her.

"Pala Mir."

A flicker of reason overcame her terror. "All right . . . Where can we go?"

"The crowd is doubling back. They're after *you*, specifically. Why?"

"I don't know. The White Rajah—my grandfather—"

"I thought he was tolerated by the people here."

"I'm not so sure, now."

It was a hundred yards down to the canal where it debouched into the Pasangara River among warehouses and shanties. The mob had flowed all the way down there and was now coming back. A few of the angry, half-naked men were searching the banks with their torches, while others darted in and out of the alleys that bordered the klong. Durell started to swim toward the open river, keeping Pala Mir's head above the surface. Their progress was slow. He managed to maneuver her closer to the opposite bank away from the crowd, where the houses cast deep shadows over the water. It was here that he spotted movement again.

It was a sampan, cautiously moving toward them.

The man in the stern lifted his pole with care, and the little boat moved slowly, keeping to the shadows.

"Tuan? Mr. Durell?"

The whisper was barely audible above the distant shouting. Durell measured the water between himself and the slowly drifting craft. Pala Mir could not make it. And now the men with torches were running along the canal bank directly opposite them, shouting to each other.

"Tuan? Quickly!"

He struck out, trying to keep from making a splash in the water. He had his fingers coiled in Pala Mir's hair, and she turned sinuously, floating on her back, giving herself up to him completely. The sampan drew closer. There was a deeper area of shadow, then a shaft of moonlight struck down between the nearby houses. From far away came the roaring of Army trucks, a military whistle, and he wondered which danger was greater—from the Malays, searching frenziedly for a victim, or from Colonel Tileong and his lieutenant, Parepa.

"Here, *tuan.*"

The face and voice were familiar. It was Chiang Gi. The old fisherman grunted as he caught Durell's forearm and hauled him upward out of the water.

"The girl first, Chiang."

"Yes, certainly, *tuan.*"

The white-haired Malay pulled Pala Mir up out of the canal with one strong heave of his powerful shoulders. The girl gasped and fell over the gunwale. The sampan rocked and splashed dangerously; then she tumbled inward and Durell followed, grateful to get out of the murky canal water. Chiang Gi fought for a moment to keep the boat steady, poling it into the deep shadows of a near-by house on the klong. Long, rippling red reflections from the torches of the mob followed them into the blackness.

"Tuan?"

"I'm all right."

"Miss Pala Mir is bleeding badly."

Durell looked across the canal. The people there were

still searching for them, for their rescue by the sampan had gone undetected. They were spreading back toward the bridge in long running waves of angry men, and the shouting now reflected their frustration. They felt cheated. At the same time, an armored car appeared at the opposite end of the bridge, and the dull thump of a three-inch cannon shook the night air. There were screams and curses and a backward surge of people. The cannon-fire was directed into the air. A machine gun rattled, and this came lower over the heads of the mob. Uniformed militia ran across the bridge with bayonets fixed. The mob hesitated, faced up to the armed men for a moment, and then, suddenly yielding to panic, exploded in every direction as its components became individuals again, intent on saving their own skins.

"They are late, as usual," Chiang Gi observed.

"I'm still grateful," Durell said. "Can you hide us, Chiang?"

"You can stay aboard the sampan until sunrise. It would be best. The militia is angry now, and they will shoot anyone they see breaking the curfew. My son-in-law, who is a friend of Colonel Tileong's secretary, says that more blood will flow unless the looting and the murders stop."

Durell nodded and turned to Pala Mir, as Chiang Gi poled the sampan down the klong. The girl sat with her back against the tiny, plaited cabin wall amidships in the little boat. Her breathing was almost regular now, less of an exercise against imminent death. He knelt beside her and pushed her wet hair from her eyes. Her head remained bowed. One breast was bare, exposed through her torn dress, and he took the wet material and covered it. She shuddered from head to foot and folded her hands in her lap. Otherwise, she did not seem to be aware of him or her surroundings.

"Pala Mir?"

"Yes."

"This is Durell. Can you understand me?"

"My arm hurts," she whispered.

"I'll fix it."

"Why did they want to kill *me?*" she asked, her voice like that of a puzzled child.

"I don't know. They wanted to kill anyone. A mob like that is like a mindless animal."

"They wanted to kill *me!*" she insisted in a louder voice. "I was only going to see my grandfather. I had to. I have no place to stay. I had to run through the jungle because they came up the river after me and burned my house and killed Tatzi—"

"Your dog?"

"Yes. Tatzi. They cut off his head and put it on a pole. Then they burned the house. I was alone in it. I jumped out of a window. I wanted to get to the convent, where the Sisters are, but I couldn't. I was afraid. I ran through the jungle to the beach, and they followed me. They shouted and cursed my name and called me a witch, a wicked woman. I'm not, Sam, I'm not! It is all lies. Paul knows they are lies, but he does not deny them. Oh, how my arm hurts!"

She spoke like a child in short, breathy sentences, her eyes blank, staring at something beyond him that no one but her could visualize.

"Did you recognize anyone in the mob, Pala Mir?"

"What do you mean?"

"Did you see anyone there who might have had any reason for turning the mob against you?"

"Who would do such a thing in Pasangara?" she asked puzzledly.

"Someone did it."

"Who?" she repeated.

He silently turned to her wounded arm. A knife had laid the flesh open, but it looked worse than it was. She would need some antibiotics to prevent infection, he thought. Perhaps a few stitches. He did the best he could, tearing his wet shirt off at the hem, making a rough bandage that pulled the lips of the wound together, then tying it securely. He wet his handkerchief in the water of the klong and washed her bloody hand, arm, and face. She sat unresisting, empty of all thought for the moment. But then she smiled.

"You are kind, Sam Durell."

"Nonsense."

"They told me that you were a terrible man, a very dangerous man."

"Who told you that?"

"My dear brother. And Colonel Tileong. I was ordered not to see you, but I—"

"Why did you try to find me?"

"I couldn't get to the Rajah. I was lost in the city, and the mob found me again and chased me."

"You know of Hammond's apartment?"

"Oh, yes."

"How did you know?"

"Paul once mentioned it," she said flatly.

"You're sure of that? Paul knows of the place?"

"He laughed about it. He said poor old Hammond was making a fool of himself with Lily Fan. He said Lily Fan was just making use of poor old Hammond."

"I see."

He remembered the rifle shots that had been aimed at him when he was swimming in the canal. No one in the mob was armed with a rifle. He remembered standing in the apartment window above the Chinese shop and having a clear view of the bridge, the sampans, and the surface of the canal.

Chiang Gi brought the boat to a halt.

12

THEY were tied up in a little cove among the docks and warehouses of the waterfront. Everything was dark and silent. Durell told Pala Mir to go into the cabin, and then he jumped ashore and walked with Chiang Gi along the dock. A small freighter was moored in the fairway, its lights blinking. He wasn't sure if it was Japanese or Russian; its lines were clean, streamlined, and modern. The lights made colored ripples on the surface of the river. Some of the fires had burned out in Chungsu, close at hand, but there were still constant sounds of people fighting the flames, a low restless murmuring like a disturbed colony of bees or wasps.

The dock led him between two long sheds and then to a street littered with waterfront debris, broken crates, a parked truck, a padlocked rack of bicycles. The moon was gone now and only the starlight gave illumination. The smells of the harbor were accented by the windless, humid night. Durell sweated. He paused beside Chiang Gi and heard an engine running; then an Army truck came down the street, dropping off patrols in two's and three's.

Chiang Gi made a clucking sound. "They are tightening the curfew. You must stay here."

"And you?" Durell asked.

"I will be all right. I have friends everywhere. I am neither Malay nor Chinese, remember, but Colonel Tileong is hunting especially for you, *tuan*. And perhaps for the girl, Pala Mir. By morning when the curfew is lifted, it may be safe for you to leave, but you should remain on the boat for tonight with the young woman."

Before Durell could stop him, the old fisherman stepped out into the street. From the shadows, Durell watched the nearest patrol whirl and descend on Chiang Gi, barking angry questions, prodding him with their bayonets. Chiang Gi replied in a whining, humble manner, but they kicked him and sent him stumbling. He fell on all fours, and the patrol laughed, picked him up, and shoved him on down the street toward Chungsu, shouting warnings after him.

In a moment the old man was out of sight.

The sampan was tied to a bollard at the end of the waterfront pier. In the reflections cast by the moored freighter in the middle of the river, Durell found a wooden ladder, climbed down the slats, looked under the wharf, and found enough headroom there in the darkness. It would be hot and stifling under there but safe enough. He untied the sampan and shoved it under the stringer, jumped into it on the forward end and used the pole to securely drive the little boat out of sight under the pier. Having tied it up again, he climbed back up the ladder to study the long pier for several moments. One of the patrols had settled down for its night's watch at the far end, where the pier joined the street. The warehouses all seemed securely locked. There was no choice. He went back down into the sampan and joined Pala Mir in the darkness of the little cabin.

"Sam?"

"It's all right. We have to stay here."

"For how long?"

"Until dawn."

She was silent. He could see little of her, except for the dim light that came across the river from the freighter and penetrated the loosely woven bamboo plaiting of the cabin walls. There was a smell of charcoal, rice, incense, and sweat in the cabin. Pala Mir smelled of lemons when he brushed her shoulder. There were two straw pallets, an iron charcoal cooker, some nets in the forward corner. Pala Mir sat with her knees drawn up to her chin, hugging her legs. Her eyes shone intermittently in the rays of light that came from the ship in the channel. She watched his every move.

"Get out of your wet clothes," Durell suggested. "I'm going to do the same. I have to dry my gun, too."

"Will it work?"

"I hope I won't need it."

"Would you use it if you have to?"

"Yes," he said quietly.

He stripped off his torn, wet shirt, his trousers, his sodden shoes, and placed them in the after cockpit of the sampan to dry. In the darkness he took apart the P-38 while sitting outside the little cabin, his head ducked to keep from bumping against the joists and stringers of the pier which sheltered them. It was like a warm, humid cave with only the lapping of the water and an occasional rocking of the sampan to let them know where they really were. He found a coolie's jacket and used it to dry the components of the Walther; then he put the gun together again by his sense of touch. It took more than fifteen minutes before he was finished. No sounds had come from the cabin behind him.

"Are you hungry?" he asked.

She sighed a little. "It seems ridiculous—but, yes, I am."

"There's a little cold rice. I think Chiang Gi must have left it for us."

They sat side by side in the tiny cabin and ate the rice. There was a bottle of wine, too. He remembered a picnic in the Litchfield Hills of Connecticut when he was at Yale; he could not remember the girl's face. It had been in the summer, and he had flown up from the heat of the Louisiana delta, where he had visited his Grandpa Jonathan. The cool green of the Connecticut hills made him feel as if the whole sky were air-conditioned. This picnic here was a bit different.

"Sam, I'm cold," Pala Mir whispered.

It was stifling in the cabin. "It's just the shock," he said quietly. "Your wound and those people who chased you—"

"Yes, perhaps. But I'm shivering."

He put his arm around her. It was true. She had taken off her torn, wet clothing, and her skin slid along his side like cool silk.

After a moment she said, "You frighten me."

"I didn't think that was really possible. You're a very brave girl."

"What you mean is that I've 'been around.' It's all on the record, isn't it? I'm such a bad girl, they say."

"I don't believe it," he told her.

"Why shouldn't you? All the newspaper stories about me—but perhaps you didn't read them all, since they were in the European newspapers." She sighed. "The Peking authorities, when I was chosen to represent the women of Pasangara at that silly propaganda convention there, remarked on my 'decadent, bourgeois, irresponsible past.'"

"You had two unfortunate marriages," he said.

"Oh, yes. Not unfortunate, though. Stupid. But you don't want to hear about them, do you?"

"No," he said.

"I tried so hard. Grandpapa was anxious to get some money to make the Merrydale name respectable again. And I only succeeded in dirtying it, they say. But I—" She paused. "If only Paul would let it all drop, instead of always reminding the poor old man about it."

"Does your grandfather still call himself the White Rajah?"

"Oh, yes. It's a question of pride. He lives in the past. Most people think he's—odd. Senile. Paul insists he should be put away because the Rajah's pretensions to royalty might irk the local people and turn them against him, and Paul is very anxious to become a solid part of Pasangara. Paul is a very solid citizen," she said bitterly.

"I thought twins always got along very well."

"Paul hates me," she said.

"And you?"

"I don't know how I feel about him. If he keeps on hurting Grandpapa, though, I—"

She was silent again. They lay side by side on the

straw pallets. Her skin was still cold but she no longer shivered. She gave a little sigh and turned on her hip toward him. The ribbon of light across the river outlined the full curves of her body.

"I would have been dead now but for you," she whispered. "Those people would have killed me. I couldn't have run any farther—"

"Don't think about it."

"You are a strange man, Sam Durell."

"Why?"

"Don't you want me? Here we are, alone, naked—"

"Yes."

"Yes, what?"

"I want you."

She laughed. "But you think I would be better off if I slept and rested? I almost slept forever an hour ago. I was almost killed but I'm still alive. Do you think I am young and beautiful?"

"Yes."

"But a 'bad girl'?"

"No."

"Could you not love me—a little?"

He was only human.

13

HE dreamed that the sampan was moving, but then he awoke and knew it was not a dream, for when he opened his eyes, he saw that dawn had brightened the Pasangara River. He heard booted footsteps on the planking of the pier overhead and a curt, military order. He turned and looked for Pala Mir on the adjacent pallet in the little cabin.

She was gone. And his gun was gone, too.

He had not heard her leave, and he felt dismayed that he had slept so soundly and had felt secure enough not to be aware of her movements. His clothes had dried partly, and he had time to get into them while the voices and the boots went on overhead. But in the meantime someone was trying to fish the sampan out from under the pier.

The hot dawn sunlight was blinding as the sampan was pulled out into the cove between the warehouses. Durell stepped out of the cabin and looked up into the muzzle of a gun held by Colonel Tileong.

Tileong looked very pleased with himself.

"Ah, Mr. Durell! What an odd place to find you!"

"A coincidence, I'm sure," Durell said.

"Completely. A routine search of the waterfront. And what do I find? The mysterious American who has been at the heart of our local difficulties ever since arrival here."

"I didn't start your riots," Durell said.

"How can we be sure? Everything is so unsettled." Tileong lowered his gun a little. "Please climb up the ladder. Do not be—ah—adventurous, now."

"Am I under arrest?"

"Yes. Certainly. This time, yes."

"May I call the consulate?"

"No. Later, perhaps. Now, no."

Lieutenant Parepa bulked hugely behind the dapper little figure of the colonel. His wide mouth grinned. He carried an automatic rifle at his hip, pointed at Durell, as Durell climbed out of the sampan and up the slats of the ladder to the deck of the pier. There were other militiamen there and a black Humber sedan. He did not see Pala Mir. Either she had betrayed him, for reasons of her own, or it had been someone else; he hadn't been found here by accident. He briefly considered Chiang Gi, Paul Merrydale, and George Hammond. He saw that the freighter that had been anchored in the river during the night was gone. Staining the bright morning sky, smoke made a muddy pall over the Chungsu area. Otherwise, the sounds on the docks and the nearby streets were normal.

"Get in the car, please," said Tileong.

Durell did not argue. He started into the back seat, but Parepa nudged him with the muzzle of his automatic rifle, so he got into the front instead. Parepa slid behind the driver's wheel. Tileong and a noncom got in the back. They took off as if Tileong were in a hurry.

He expected to be taken to the towering white government building that dominated the town, but the Humber was directed the other way through the mean slums of Chungsu and out along a deserted, weed-grown boulevard that presently skirted the swampy coast. The sun that rose over the sea was malevolent with its heat and brilliance. Parrots flashed across the empty, deserted paving, and he saw monkeys swinging in the trees. Sea birds hovered over the beach. A fishing village offered no signs of life. The boulevard, obviously long neglected, became bumpy; the asphalt and occasional patches of concrete were heaved, cracked, and broken. Durell began to worry as the town was left miles behind.

"Where are you taking me?" he asked.

"My headquarters," said Tileong.

"I must notify my consulate."

"They will be informed that you have been taken into custody for a violation of the curfew and for inciting disturbances in the city."

"What about a lawyer?"

"Pasangara is under martial law. All civil rights have been temporarily revoked by order of Premier Kuang."

The weedy, dilapidated boulevard ended nowhere, five miles south of the town. There were mangrove swamps, and a warm wind blew from over the South China Sea that stretched in green placidity to the eastern horizon. A bit of white sand beach was lined with coconut palms. Parepa bumped the Humber off the end of the boulevard and headed into the hard-packed sand. They slewed a little, the rear wheels spun, and then they splashed through shallow sea water. Another road began a half mile further on. Durell noted there had been no other car tracks on the beach.

Presently he saw the steel web of a radio tower above the palms and mangroves. Then the road improved, and they circled inland and came out again on a second beach where an old Martello-type fort, built of bricks used as ship ballast in former years, stood facing the sea. The fort was overgrown with weeds and vines and looked a century old. The provincial flag flew from a staff at the entrance.

Parepa stopped the car.

Durell felt Tileong tap his shoulder, so he got out of the Humber and stood in the breathless morning heat, facing the glitter of the sea. There were bicycles racked at the fort entrance, and a militiaman armed with a rifle saluted as Tileong approached. There were other soldiers here, and as he walked through the tunnel-like entrance, he glimpsed a radio room that went with the modern steel tower over the fort. He knew that whatever the situation in Pasangara, Tileong had personal communication with the capital and perhaps anywhere else in the world.

"Please enter my office," Tileong said.

There had to be a generator to provide independent power for the radio here. There was a desk, a narrow slot of a window that faced the sea, and a deep embrasure where an old cannon had once been sited. Two wooden chairs stood against the damp, mossy brick wall. A map of the province was framed on the opposite wall. Over the desk was a portrait of a smiling, roly-poly Chinese of genial countenance, and Durell recognized it as Premier Kuang, governmental chief of Pasangara. The militia guard went away, and Parepa stood by the door while Tileong seated himself behind his desk. The desk was very clean, except for a single folder set in the middle of the green blotter, and Tileong used his carefully manicured hands to square the folder neatly before he sighed and lit a cigarette.

He did not offer Durell one or ask him to sit down. Durell took one of the wooden chairs, anyway.

Tileong said, "I would like to be civilized about all this, Mr. Durell."

"Of course. What is this place?"

"My headquarters. Security Station Five."

"Convenient and private," Durell observed.

"Oh, yes. I do my most important work here. This fort was built by the White Rajah, the old man who still lives in Pasangara. It was a long time ago. It is useful."

"For rubber hose techniques?"

"I told you," Tileong said gently, "I would like to be decent about this. Are you hungry?"

"I've had no breakfast, as you know."

"It will be attended to presently. We will have coffee soon. Are you thirsty?"

"Yes."

"Well, presently. I am hurried for time. It will depend on you and how you give me the information I need."

"Is this an official interrogation?" Durell asked.

"You may call it that." Tileong opened the folder, looked at it, and then stared out through the slot in the embrasure and studied the sea, as if he were searching for something out there on its dazzling green surface. Tileong's smooth brown face looked as if he had not slept for several nights. His narrow little moustache needed trimming. He said, "We would like to know, in all truthfulness and in all detail, just what you are doing here in Pasangara at this particular time, Mr. Durell."

"I have been assigned as assistant legal secretary to Mr. Condon, the American consul."

Tileong said smoothly, "Yes, and we are very interested in the reason why the Central Intelligence Agency of the United States considers Pasangara of such interest as to send you to assist Mr. George Hammond in whatever project he is working on."

Durell was silent.

"Do you deny being an agent of the CIA?"

"Of course I deny it."

"You are being extremely foolish, sir." Tileong opened and closed the folder without looking at it. "How did you happen to find Miss Pala Mir?"

"A fine young woman."

"Did you make love to her during the night?"

"That's quite a personal question."

"I apologize. Was she very frightened by the unfortunate incident which overtook her?"

"Of course."

"Have you met old Anthony Merrydale, our White Rajah?" Tileong did not smile.

"No."

"A most interesting gentleman. How long have you known Mr. George Hammond?"

"Many years. He's an old friend."

"And Lily Fan?"

"Don't know her."

"You met her last night, did you not?"

"No," Durell said.

Tileong sighed. "Mr. Durell, I cannot remain too long away from Pasangara. The violence there is growing. I have so little time. Do you like our climate here, by the way?"

"It reminds me a little of home."

"Ah, yes. What is your province? Louisiana? Delta country, I believe, much like Pasangara's."

Durell felt hungry and thirsty, but he knew Tileong's ploy, so he sat quietly, watching the sea through the fort's embrasure. A telephone rang somewhere and then rang again on Tileong's desk. He answered it in quick Malay, his black eyes regarding Durell blankly, as if he weren't really there. Durell looked at the portrait of Premier Kuang. After a moment, Tileong hung up and then stood, short and very neat in his uniform.

"I must go. I will ask you once more: what is your business in Pasangara? I assure you, I would make every effort to cooperate with you, if possible. I am not your enemy. You do have enemies here, that is true; but I am not one of them. Nevertheless, I have my duty to perform, and I will take every step to learn the truth, whatever the cost may be."

"To hell with you," Durell said.

"Very well. I will leave the rest of the questions to Lieutenant Parepa."

Parepa spoke only basic English. His methods were equally basic. He enjoyed his work and went at it with a gusto that perhaps exceeded Colonel Tileong's orders.

"You tell me truth now," he grunted.

"Let's get Mr. Condon, the consul, over here."

"Nobody help you. You all mine."

"You must believe in Santa Claus," Durell said.

"Who he?"

"Never mind. It would take too long to explain."

"Have much time. You talk. I listen."

Parepa used his rubber truncheon this time. The first blow slammed across the side of Durell's head and knocked him out of the chair. He came up with his head ringing and his vision blurred but aimed his fist at Parepa's belly. Parepa stepped back and laughed.

"Not here. Colonel like his furniture. We break nothing here. Come."

There was a small cell in the back of the brick fort. It had no windows, and it smelled of palm rats, the sea, and death. A single faint bulb hung from a wire overhead, naked and garish. There was no furniture at all. A massive steel-grilled gate was the only way in or out, and two guards, who looked fairly alert, stood out in the dank corridor with their weapons ready.

Parepa knew his business and was perfectly single-minded about it. Durell soon lost track of time. He was aware of pain, of blood in his mouth, of a useless hand hanging limply from what felt like a broken wrist. He could see only dimly. Once or twice he passed out and was vaguely aware of the cool stone floor, a blessing in the sullen heat that encompassed the fort and the beach. He tried to keep these periods of lying inert as long as possible, but Parepa was difficult to fool. The questions went on and on.

"You with CIA?"

"Never heard of it."

"What is K Section?"

"Don't know."

"What your business here?"

"Tourist."

"You lie." Pause. "You with consulate?"

"Right. Chalk one up for you. Call them."

"How you work with Pala Mir? She Communist? Why you work with her, hey?"

"She's a wonderful girl."

"Her brother fine man. She bad girl. Old Rajah bad man, eh?"

"Never met the old gentleman."

"You son-bitch, you lie to Parepa?"

"Never, buddy."

More pain, darkness, and strange whirling lights behind his eyes. He did not fight back. Deep in his mind, a warning glowed and held steady. Parepa wanted to kill him. You didn't give him the opportunity or the excuse. Hang on. You last long enough, maybe Tileong will come back. Not much help there, though. Pain in the left hand, pain behind the eyes. An image of George Hammond, a human wreck after East Germany, drifted into his mind and chilled his heart. He didn't want to end up like George Hammond. And George had been lucky. Maybe. They let him live. Parepa meant to kill him. Maybe you could kill Parepa first.

Durell became a cunning animal, remembering how to ease the blows, to roll with them, to go with the twists and wrenches of limbs and torso. Parepa was panting. He was big but there was some blubber on him. Parepa sweated. There was a pause, and Parepa howled at one of the guards, who hurried away and presently came back with a mug of tea. Parepa leaned against the brick wall, drank the tea with sucking noises, and looked at

Durell, who had let himself be thrown into the corner like a pile of old rags.

"Lots time," Parepa said. "You like tea?"

"I prefer coffee."

"Hungry?"

"No. I need some bicarb."

"Hey?"

"I have a stomach ache."

Parepa laughed.

He slept. He dreamed bad dreams. The light that hung by its wire from the ceiling did not go out. He was alone, and he could not see the guards through the grilled gate to the fortress cell, but he could hear them talking somewhere. He could hear, too, the sound of the sea on the beach and the sudden squawk of a parrot and then, surprisingly, a volley of shots, and then another volley. The jungle around them went very silent. Durell stared up at the glowing light bulb. It seemed very dim, and it was difficult to judge its distance because one eye was closed, his left one, since Parepa seemed to favor it for his knuckles. At least he hadn't gouged it out with his thumb. The wire was long enough. If you jumped high enough, you might tear it loose from the ceiling. Then tie it around your throat and tie it to something else in the ceiling. But the arching bricks had nothing to fasten it to. You didn't want to end up like George Hammond, broken in body and spirit. Better the wire and quick strangulation.

Parepa came in again.

"You have good rest, CIA man?"

"Lovely."

"You talk now?"

"Anything you say."

"Good. What you do in Pasangara?"

"When the U.S. Marines land, you'll find out."

Parepa laughed. He was very amused. "Once upon time, yes. Not today. Time change. No Marines for you. World is different. Washington no care what happen to

American citizen now. Everybody spit on them, if they like."

"That's right. Nobody likes to be in debt."

"I spit on you, see?"

Durell wiped it off his face.

Parepa said, "I get tape recorder, you talk now, I get doctor, fix you up good as new, hey?"

"The doctor is a good idea."

"So you talk? Drink tea? Good rice? Rest and then go home."

"No dancing girls?"

Parepa frowned. "You son-bitch."

Presently Durell felt himself hurled into deep blackness again.

He awoke once more and kept his eyes closed, then heard a cultivated voice say, "It is inhuman what you have done to this man, Lieutenant Parepa. I do not care how stubborn he may be, we do not treat prisoners this way in Pasangara. Get the doctor down here, please, and do hurry. I will discuss this matter with you and Colonel Tileong later."

"He prisoner. Security. No answer questions."

"Never mind. Get the doctor."

Durell opened his eyes. He thought for a moment he was back in Tileong's office in the fort, looking at the portrait of Premier Kuang hanging on the wall. But this was Kuang in the flesh. Lots of it. The premier was a regular Humpty-Dumpty of a Chinese, round of face and belly, with kindly, concerned eyes, a jovial smile, an intelligent brow, and a gentle manner. Behind the eyes there might be something else, but Durell was not concerned about that for the moment.

"Ah, you are awake, sir?"

"Somewhat."

"The doctor will be here in a moment. I must apologize for what happened. It was all a terrible mistake."

"Am I to be released?" Durell asked.

"We will discuss that after the doctor comes."

"Let me go now. I'll walk back to town."

"That would be unthinkable, sir."

The doctor came. He was a Chinese, too. Durell's mouth was clotted with blood, there was a cut inside his cheek, and his wrist needed taping; but nothing was broken. The doctor swabbed at his eye, made little hissing noises of consolation, dived into his bag of ointments, applied them, and took out a hypodermic syringe.

"No needle," Durell said promptly.

"But it will help with the pain."

"I happen to feel fine."

"You must have a sedative, sir."

"No, thanks."

Durell tried to stand up. He fell down, tried again, got to his feet, and leaned against the brick wall of the cell. Premier Kuang, in a fine silk suit of sky blue, watched him with interest. He should have felt flattered by Kuang's presence here, but it served only to alarm him. His ribs ached along his left side. When he felt them, the doctor hurried over to poke and prod, nod and hiss. Then he got more surgical tape and applied it with expert, careful hands. It was easier to breathe then.

"You really must have a sedative at once, sir," the doctor insisted.

"Let me see the vial."

"Of course."

It was a ten cc. bottle of Demerol. The syringe held only one cc. Durell nodded and let the doctor inject him. He hoped the label hadn't been faked or a different solution been injected in the vial; he didn't think they would go to that extreme here. He sat down on the floor again.

Premier Kuang said, "You have become acquainted with my daughter, I understand. Lily Fan is a lovely girl but rather high-spirited and independent. She has forgotten the old ways of filial respect. I am most distressed by her relationship with your friend George Hammond."

"I can understand that."

Kuang gave Durell his Humpty-Dumpty smile. "It

is plain from what Colonel Tileong tells me that you have not made his work simpler. I am only concerned with peace in Pasangara and reaching an end to our civil riots. We have democracy here, sir, as you can see from the fact that although I am premier, I am also Chinese, elected by a Malay majority. It is necessary, Mr. Durell, to remove you from my jurisdiction. We will take you back to your hotel where you may rest undisturbed, I assure you, and although the airfield has been damaged by subversives and Pao Thet terrorists who took advantage of the rioting—"

"What Pao Thet terrorists?"

"All of Southeast Asia is riddled by Communist guerrilla groups, as you surely know, from Burma and Thailand on down through this province far to the south. Pasangara has certainly not been spared their attention. It is like a plague, but I am most determined to contain it. I shall crush these so-called Pao Thets, sir. Given a minor fever, such as our present disturbances, the plague spreads and seizes on our vital organs and tries to destroy all that we have so painfully achieved to this date. I will not let that happen. When the airfield is repaired, you will be flown out of Pasangara. I truly regret this necessity."

Durell began to feel sleepy.

14

HE awoke in his room at the Kuan Diop Hotel. The doors to the veranda overlooking the river allowed a warm breeze to come in. It was night, and only a dim light shone in one corner of the room. He was alone.

He remembered vaguely riding in the premier's limousine with Kuang, polite, attentive, and solicitous, but with something behind his intelligent eyes that Durell could not make out. He was acutely aware that no one, at any time, had mentioned the missing U.S. Navy Thrashers.

He ached from head to foot and he was hungry and thirsty. He still had his watch; it read 10:30. He sat up with an effort and used the phone to order dinner, which was promised in half an hour. Then he stripped off the bandages the Chinese doctor had applied and managed to get himself into the huge bathroom to step under the shower. Electric power had returned to Pasangara but not peace. Through the bathroom window he could see new fires burning in Chungsu, glowing red against the night.

The shower water was tepid, neither cool nor refreshing. He stood under it for a long time, then managed to shave, slowly feeling the aches and stiffness leave his limbs. By the time he was dressed again, a skirted male servant of the Kuan Diop staff rolled in a dinner of *satay*, bits of meat grilled on bamboo skewers, and a *rojak* salad of bean sprouts, chili, mashed peanuts, and fish paste. He ate with surprising relish.

He wanted nothing more than to roll into bed and sleep for twelve hours; but he knew he couldn't do that.

The troops were gone from around the hotel, and when he looked into the corridor, no one was guarding his door. Beyond the veranda in the waterfront park, the old paddlewheel steamer was being loaded by slow-moving stevedores under spotlights.

Feeling better, he ate slowly and took a long drink from his depleted bottle of bourbon. He noted that the bug he had removed from his telephone had been replaced. He left it there and phoned the consulate. David Condon was out, according to the night secretary. So was George Hammond. He was just hanging up when the consul himself knocked on the door.

Mr. Condon, with his long blond hair, blue eyes, and finely chiseled face, looked like a modern Shelley. His white suit must have been especially tailored for him in one of San Francisco's mod shops. He looked elegant but angry and spoke perfunctorily. "May I come in?"

"You *are* in," Durell said. "Sit down. I've been trying to reach you. I need some help."

"Indeed. *My* help! See here, Durell, or whatever your name really is—"

"It's Samuel C. Durell."

"—I've had nothing but complaints from the government about you ever since you arrived. I told you when you first came here, I would tolerate no disturbances to my relationship with the local regime, but you've gone ahead in total disregard of my wishes to maintain a good rapport with Premier Kuang and his people here—"

"To coin a phrase," Durell said, "you can't make an omelet without breaking eggs. Sit down. Have a drink."

Condon was suspicious. "Do you drink much? Is that why you look so—so—whatever happened to your face?"

"I was interrogated by Colonel Tileong."

Condon stared haughtily. "Yes, I know. But why?"

"I have a job to do," Durell said patiently. "If it can be done quietly, fine. But sometimes it seems as if everybody knows everything that goes on in your consulate. Your security level is pretty low."

"That's George Hammond's job."

"I know."

"And you're supposed to work with Hammond. I don't have any real directives about you, Durell. I suppose you're here from one of the agencies, but it's not up to me to cater to your trouble-making schemes—"

"No schemes," Durell said quietly. "I'm just trying to find twelve missing Navy Thrashers."

Condon was pretty good about it. He sat down, pulled up his carefully creased white trousers, and adjusted the wide necktie he wore under his Edwardian lapels. He smoothed his long hair over his ears on each side of his young head, coughed, and looked at Durell.

"The Thrashers. Yes. I see."

"The Navy asked you to look into them, too."

"Are you from ONI?" Condon asked.

"Not exactly."

"A parallel agency?"

"You might say so."

Condon spoke petulantly. "I wish you had told me so right in the beginning. It's all a stupid false alarm. I don't know what happened to them, but to imagine they've been lured all the way across the South China Sea to this out-of-the-way province is ridiculous. I know nothing about them."

"Didn't you hear them?"

"I beg your pardon."

"I heard two going over last night." Durell was surprised to realize that little more than twenty-four hours had passed since he had been chased through the jungle on his way to Pala Mir's river house. "You have no data on them?"

Condon got up nervously, walked around the room, and looked out on the veranda. "I think this place is bugged. Colonel Tileong is pretty efficient."

"He is. Tileong knows all about it."

"I can't make that man out. He makes me nervous."

"He makes me hurt," said Durell.

Condon ignored that. "I don't know if he's behind the subversive guerrilla movement that recently started these riots in town or not."

"I thought you thought *I* started them," said Durell.

Condon stood up. "Let's go for a walk. In the park down there. We can talk more freely."

"I think not. It's safer here in some ways. I just want you to send a message for me to Kuala Lumpur. We have a man in our embassy there that I want to contact."

"Hammond is supposed to do that."

"I'd rather do it myself through you. How is your memory?"

"Fine," said Condon. "Give me the message."

"It goes to Mr. Smith at our K.L. establishment. Simply say, 'Hennessy flying solo. Send data mongoose soonest to Jones. Also new RDF-Mark IX. Regards to Susie from Jasper.'"

Condon looked blank. "What does all that mean? Are you Hennessy, Jones, or Jasper?"

"Can you send it tonight?"

"Yes, we have our own radio communications—"

"Fine. That's all, then."

He had only a ten-minute respite before his second visitor arrived. There was a light tap on the door, and he came back from the veranda where he had been watching the riverboat and opened it, stepping a little to one side as he did so in case the visitor was unfriendly. He could not have been further wrong. It was Lily Fan.

Tiny, delicate, yet infinitely a woman, Lily tripped in wearing a Western minidress of flowered silk with her sleek black hair cut simply in front but dressed regally above her proud little head. Her whole manner was tremulous, as if she were ready to take flight simply at an angry look or word.

"Mr. Durell, I hope you don't mind my visiting you at this late hour—"

"I don't mind. But is it wise?"

"Oh, it's all right. Daddy—the premier—knows I've gone to see you. In fact, he suggested it. He also sends further apologies for your treatment."

"What excuse did you give for seeing me?"

She giggled, and it might have sounded enchanting to Hammond, but Durell was not in the mood. She said, "Oh, I told him I wanted to know more about George and that you had once known him and might give me information to settle my mind about the whole thing."

"I thought it was settled already," Durell said.

"Yes, it is. I love George and he loves me. It may sound crazy to everyone, and certainly Daddy doesn't approve. He thinks I'm a terrible person, disloyal to him and to China itself; but this is a modern world, and people are doing new things every day—"

"New things for them," said Durell. "Not new for the world."

She looked blank for a moment. "Anyway, I've come to beg you to be kind to George. He—he's a little uncertain about you. He wants—so much to prove he's everything he once was."

Durell's face was like stone. He watched the Chinese girl move across the room like a long-legged colt but not without a practiced roll of the hips and a long, sidelong glance at him out of her black almond eyes. She could have won a beauty contest anywhere in the world. She had charm, good looks, the body, and the brains. He didn't trust her much farther than he could have thrown her.

"What would you like me to do about George?" he asked. "In the way of being 'kind,' that is."

She pouted. "Oh, you know."

He said, "I'm going to see to it that George is fired and pulled out of Pasangara as fast as possible," Durell said in a flat voice. "I think he's a bit insane."

She looked shocked. She turned away from the view of the river through the veranda doors, walked toward him, and then stopped, tilting her flower-like face up to his. Her mouth was open, her moist lips parted, and she seemed to have stopped breathing.

"But—why?"

"Did George really send you here, Lily?"

"No. But—oh, please, I'm so upset—"

"Where can I reach him?"

"He told me not to tell you."

"I think you had better."

She turned away, opened her beaded purse, and took out a cigarette. Her gestures were young, awkward, but very feminine. Her eyes watched him. She said, "Did Colonel Tileong hurt you very badly? Your face is badly bruised."

"Where can I reach George?" he insisted.

"Everything is so mixed up, isn't it?" She smiled, then dropped the purse, and puffed clumsily at the cigarette. "All I know is that I love him. I've loved him since we first met six months ago when I came back from school. He's fine and gentle and understanding, and I feel so sorry for him—"

"Don't confuse pity with love, Lily Fan."

"I don't. I understand about all that."

"How old are you, Lily?"

"Twenty-two."

He looked at her. She blushed.

"Well, nineteen," she said. "But it makes no difference! George and I—well, it's wonderful with us, and I don't care what people think about it. He deserves a new chance, and I'm going to help him get it." She paused. "He sent you a message. That's why I'm really here."

"Good. May I have it?"

She searched her purse again, handed him a folded slip of paper, and looked perplexed. "I tried to read it. I must confess I was curious. But it's in code. Even George couldn't read it. It came in over his radio from Taipei. He tried it on a funny little machine he has, but it didn't come out making any sense."

Durell took the paper but did not look at it. "You'd better go home. Your father will be worried about you."

She stood very close to him. Her scent was heady and exotic. She was very beautiful. She put her hands on his shoulders and folded her fingers behind his neck. He didn't like that grip, but she didn't go any farther, and perhaps she didn't mean anything by it. Her body pressed against his.

"I'd do anything to help George. Anything."

He smiled. "George wouldn't like that."

"George wouldn't have to know about it, would he?"

"Has he shown any jealousy about you?"

She shrugged, and since he did not react to the pressure of her body against him, she drew away a little but still kept her hands clasped behind his neck.

"You don't like me, do you?"

"I want two things from you, Lily. I want a telephone number where I can get George and a few moments to read this message. Are you sure he couldn't decode it?"

"He was very annoyed about it. He didn't want to send it over to you, but I told him he'd better because you might be expecting it."

He turned a little sidewise toward the light that came from the veranda, unfolded the paper, and scanned it. He had memorized the new code that McFee had given him in Taipei before he flew here, and thanks to his mnemonic training, he could read it as if it were in clear.

It was a Q/22 URGENT, citing a protest from the Pasangaran provincial government, timed 2200 hours yesterday, regarding his activities in the city. The important element in the message was a priority request for a surveillance estimate of Hammond's reliability. It was just as well that Hammond had not been able to decode it.

The last part of the message cited a crate of missing Mk. 27 Rad. Deflect devices called Boomerangs, which had been stolen two months ago from a U.S. Army Quartermaster depot in Saigon but presumably had found its way into the Vietnam black market. Detailed descriptions of the crate of Boomerangs and its markings followed.

Lily Fan pressed her small, lush body against him again, standing on tiptoe. "Is it important?" she whispered.

"No, not at all."

"Is it about George?"

"Nothing about George," he said, smiling down at her. "How long can you stay here, Lily Fan?"

"All night, if you want me."

"Where can I reach George? You must tell me."

"You won't hurt him, will you?"

"Not if I can help it."

She wriggled her hips and slid her black eyes sidewise around the room and said, "Phone 22-63-22."

"Where is that telephone located?"

"I don't know. It's where I always reach him before we meet at the apothecary's place."

"Very good, Lily. Now be a good girl and take your hands off me."

Her eyes popped wide open with surprise and chagrin. "But I thought—don't you want—"

"No, Lily. Go home."

When her grip tightened around his neck, he flexed his knees forward, bent his head, reached back, caught one of her fingers, and tried to pry her loose. She was strong and very good at it—but not good enough. She gave a small cry as his pressure threatened to break her fingers. She brought one knee up dangerously, but he turned sidewise to her, hooked the leg she rested her weight on, and flipped her backward. Her grip on his neck flew apart, and she thudded against the bed, bounced on it, and came up grabbing for her little purse. Durell reached it first. She gasped, tried to scratch him, her face transformed by fury. Nothing like a woman scorned, he thought. He backed away from her, but she came on like a little cat, snatching for the bag. Instinctively he slapped her—hard enough to throw her back on the bed again. It creaked. A spring whined. He wondered what the listeners on Colonel Tileong's mike would think of it. At the moment it didn't matter. He got the purse open and found, among cosmetics, a five-inch switch blade and a tiny, pearl-handled .28, a "husband-killer." Lily Fan was a remarkable girl.

She breathed hard, contemplating a new plan of action. Her hand groped at the buttons over her breasts. He didn't want her to scream and find himself a victim of the badger game with the girl who was the premier's daughter. He twisted her hand aside, picked her up bodily, and carried her, wriggling, to the door. Opening it, he deposited her in the outer corridor.

"You're a love, Lily Fan. But not tonight, do you understand?"

"Oh, you are a bastard," she gasped. "I've never been so insulted and humiliated—"

"I'll give the knife and gun back to George, when and
if I see him again."

He closed the door firmly in her furious face.

15

THE telephone rang four times before it was picked up.
Durell listened silently, hearing someone breathe hard for
several moments. Then Hammond's voice said:

"Yes?"

"Cajun here."

"Yes?"

"You're not surprised?"

"All right, I'm surprised."

"You thought Tileong still hád me?"

"Yes, that's what I thought."

"You didn't do much to help me," said Durell.

"There was nothing I could do."

"You could have used your influence with your future
father-in-law. After all, Premier Kuang—"

"What do you want, Cajun?"

"Boomerang devices."

"What?"

"Boomerangs. Where are they?"

"I don't know what you're talking about. It's hot and
I'm sleepy. Are you at the hotel? If so, I'll call you tomorrow. I'm going back to bed."

"Not with Lily, you won't."

"I don't—"

"She was just here with me," Durell said.

There was a long silence.

"What's all this about Boomerangs, Cajun?"

"I asked you first."

"I told you—and what was that crack about Lily?"

"She came here with your message. And she loves you enough to beg me not to do anything to hurt you, George."

"Jesus."

"And she offered to stay with me for the night."

There was a longer silence this time. Durell looked out over the veranda to the park and the little dock where the river steamer was moored. The stevedores had stopped working. The floodlights were turned out. The park looked dark and quiet. He moved back from the veranda doors so he wouldn't be seen against the light by anyone in the shrubbery. Then he reached out and turned off the single lamp in the room. The darkness felt better but hot and sticky.

Hammond said, "You're lying, Sam. She isn't like that. I know women."

"You've lost touch," Durell said. "The pill, the generation gap."

"You son of a bitch."

"I want to ask you something, George."

"To hell with you."

"From your safe house you could see me running to the canal, couldn't you?"

A pause. "Yes."

"Did you watch me?"

"For a moment."

"Two moments, George. You watched for two moments."

"What do you mean?"

"Two rifle shots were fired at me while I was swimming in the canal."

"Listen, Cajun." Hammond's voice trembled a little. "From this minute on, you're on your own."

"Then you'd better practice up on your marksmanship," Durell said.

He hung up.

16

THERE were many stories told about George Hammond among the field staff who worked out of K Section's headquarters at No. 20 Annapolis Street in Washington, D. C.

When he had been K control for Bulgaria with a front office in Sofia as a minor party official, there was an incident involving a Turk who had obtained data on the Soviet Black Sea fleet which electronic equipment had not been able to pick up. At that time, which was some years ago, Hammond had already become a deadly legend. He used a hammer-and-tongs method to achieve his goals. He had lost one agent, and another was missing somewhere down toward the Greek border, where a rendezvous had been arranged with the Turkish gentleman who had the information Hammond wanted.

The missing agent was a Levantine who had been employed occasionally by K Section on minor missions. It was soon clear to Hammond that his precarious cover had been blown by the Lebanese, that the opponent's security forces were after him, and that the Turk was in danger of falling into enemy hands.

Hammond did not waste time. He kidnapped the head of enemy security, found the traitorous Levantine, killed him, took a rubber raft into the Black Sea with the Turk, and drifted about the marshy mouths of the Danube River for two weeks, eating roots and berries, while being hunted as if he were a mad dog.

No one knew the casualties he inflicted on his opposite numbers during those two weeks. He was given top priority for execution. But somehow he turned up in Istanbul, forty pounds less, with a terrified Turk whose sense of shock had required psychiatric treatment, after a priority flight to Washington, before he could speak. When the Turk saw Hammond again, he screamed in fear. But he gave his information eventually, and Hammond, after a week in the hospital, demanded field service again.

Another story dealt with his flight to contact dissident Kurds in northeast Syria, whose government was carrying out a policy of "final solution" by exterminating the Kurdish villages through a process of denationalization, appropriation of farmlands, and population transports to desert lands. Hammond and a Kurdish chief thereupon started a small war.

Hammond's feats as a soldier of fortune were legendary. He spoke Kurdish, Arabic, and half a dozen other Middle Eastern languages, including Ivrit. His bravery was uncontested. The warlike Kurds made him a chief in his own right. He smuggled Russian-built tanks, armored cars, and infantry weapons—even two MIG-17's—from Syrian army depots in a wild escapade that helped the Kurdish tribe over the border into neighboring Iraq where, although the Iraqi government was hardly less friendly to the Kurds, they found refuge. In the course of this small war Hammond achieved a reputation similar to that of the fabled Lawrence of Arabia.

He was not a man to be taken lightly.

When Durell hung up the telephone after speaking to Hammond, he knew he had a problem.

Whatever Hammond's motives, the man was not quite rational now. His ambition to get back into the centers of agency power could not be ignored. He would tackle any obstacle in his way with cunning, trickery, and a savage knowledge of method and procedure that surpassed even Durell's own experience.

If he stood in Hammond's way, Hammond would move to eliminate him. Swiftly. Ruthlessly. With no more feeling than he had exhibited in his past work.

Durell checked out his room with extra care. He took his time about it. He turned out the light again, tapped the walls, checked the locks, and searched the bath, the toilet box, the drain pipes—anything that could be easily plugged with explosives. He walked the length of the veranda from one corner of the hotel to the other. Most of the other rooms were dark. From one he heard a radio with a taped speech of Premier Kuang's, exhorting the populace to remain calm and obey the curfew. Kuang's voice was measured and reasonable. Through another window he saw a man and a woman in their bed, a contortion of limbs and torsos that defied imagination. He passed by quietly, looked over the railing, and decided that anyone with a little agility could climb up the convenient Victorian scrollwork that fretted this entire facade.

He went back to his room and quietly unpacked his bag. From a false bottom in the suitcase, built in K Section's laboratories by the gimmick boys who delighted in elaborate and usually unworkable gadgets, he took out a small rebuilt Beretta .32, a knife, a small Thermit bomb, and a set of picklocks. His face ached, and his bruises seemed aflame from Lieutenant Parepa's recent attentions.

He had just finished when someone else knocked.

He stood still in the darkness, thinking that his biggest problem was that Hammond was equally adept in all the tricks, programs, and procedures of K Section and probably had invented a few methods of his own beyond the training program at the "Farm."

The knock was repeated lightly.

"Sam?"

Holding the Beretta ready in his right hand, he stood to one side of the door and opened it with his left.

Pala Mir slipped inside.

Durell threw the bolt behind her, crossed to close the veranda doors, and turned on the wooden ceiling fans. They created an illusion of cooler air. In the dim light he saw that Pala Mir was dressed in a dark Chinese jumper and trousers and was wearing black sneakers. A small pin glittered on her left breast. Her dark hair was pulled back into a severe bun at the nape of her neck.

"Oh, Sam, I'm glad to find you here," she said.

"No thanks to you," he said. "Where did you go while I was asleep on the sampan?"

"I couldn't help it. I thought I heard a noise, so I climbed up on the dock, but some soldiers were walking down toward the end where we were hidden. It was almost dawn." She paused. Her face, a perfect blend of all that was lovely in the East and West, was tilted up to his with concern. "Are you all right?"

"A few minor bruises, that's all."

"Was Tileong so terrible to you?"

"We were not exactly friendly. You haven't told me why you took my gun when you left me on the sampan."

She shrugged. "Oh, you are a strange man. So suspicious. I was worried about the soldiers, that is all. Sam those few hours together were so beautiful."

"Then why did you leave?"

"I had to hide in one of the warehouses. When the soldiers got between me and the sampan, I found a door that wasn't locked, and I couldn't return. It was almost dawn then, anyway. So I slipped away."

"Do you have my gun with you?"

"I left it at Grandpapa's house. The so-called palace of the White Rajah." She smiled ruefully. "I went there to hide and remained all day. He wants to see you."

"The White Rajah?"

"He's very concerned about you."

"What does he know about me?"

"Only what I told him. It's all right, Sam. He's a wonderful old man. You'll like him. And I think he'll help you, too." She paused. "Are you very angry with me?"

"No."

"You are. I can tell. Do you believe all the bad things they say about me?"

"No."

"You do. But that doesn't matter. You can believe one thing, however. I am your only friend in all of Pasangara."

"I'll buy that," Durell said.

It was midnight when they left the Kuan Diop Hotel. She had parked a Land Rover in a driveway near the service entrance by the dark shrubbery of the park, and he studied every shadow as they slipped out the back door of the hotel. She showed him a pass that allowed her to ignore the curfew. It was signed by Colonel Tileong.

The Land Rover was rigged like a safari-hunter's African bush wagon. There were two rifles in slings on each side of the interior, canteens of water, and extra fuel cans lashed to the back. Directly over the driver's seat in a fixed leather holster was a regulation Colt .45, easily reached by whoever held the wheel.

"I'll drive," said Durell.

The back area of the hotel was dark, but he was sure that eyes watched their departure. There were no troops on the boulevard tonight, and the city seemed quieter. He thought it was too quiet. The heat of the night and the lack of wind bred an ominous calm, like that before a thunderstorm. Watching the empty streets, Pala Mir sat far over on her side of the seat, her face impassive. Now and then she gave him directions to turn right or left.

Chungsu was on the north bank of the river. When they crossed a steel girder bridge, they met the first military checkpoint. Pala Mir showed the corporal her pass; the soldier stared hard at Durell, then waved them on.

The old Chinese settlement on the north bank of the Pasangara was quite different from the more modern city on the opposite side of the river. The streets were narrow and twisting, the houses higher and hedged in shoulder-to-shoulder. Devious little alleys, too small for anything but a pedicab or bicycle, led away into dark cul-de-sacs. The evidence of the riots was more plainly to be seen here.

"Go to the end of the street, then to the waterfront," Pala Mir said distantly. "That is, if you trust me."

"I suppose I must," Durell said.

"I thought that you and I—after last night—" She paused and laughed, her manner brittle. "Well, I've had two husbands, and I shouldn't talk like a schoolgirl, should I?"

"Do you feel like one?" he asked.

She hesitated. "Somehow, yes. With you."

"Why does the Rajah want to see me?"

"He'll tell you about it. You mustn't be at all surprised at how he looks and lives. The past is his hobby, practically an obsession. That's why Paul claims he is senile or losing his wits." Her voice grew bitter. "But it isn't so, Sam. He's a dear old man who's making a great effort to keep up with the times, with the new democracy. He's very loyal to the regime—and worried about it."

"No secret ambition to become a rajah again?"

"You can make up your own mind about that."

As he drove the vehicle slowly among the potholes and debris that still littered the streets of Chungsu, he told her about his own Grandfather Jonathan, that fine old gentleman who lived in Bayou Peche Rouge in Louisiana aboard the hulk of his river steamboat. Pala Mir listened with greater interest than he had expected.

"And you love the old man?" she asked.

"Of course. He taught me most of what I know."

"I'm glad," she said simply. "Perhaps that will make it easier."

He turned as she directed, and they came out on a broad waterfront road of docks and wharves facing the open harbor. The oil tanker was still moored out there. A small freighter showed its lights a few hundred yards down the way, and he wondered if it were the same he had seen in the river last night. The moon silvered the horizon of the sea.

"There," said Pala Mir. "That's the old palace. It's

really a fort and warehouse that the first Anthony Merry-dale, the original White Rajah, built when he landed here."

Stark and ominous against the pattern of moonlight, the place was built of dark stone with a crenelated tower and narrow windows, silhouetted on a slender point of land thrust into the harbor. The long esplanade facing the sea was empty. One of the nearby warehouses had been burned to the ground, and the smell of rank, charred stuff was still strong in the midnight air. Being on the waterfront brought no relief from the stifling, silent heat.

Durell stopped the Land Rover in the shadows of the burned building. He reached up over the driver's wheel and took the Colt .45 from its holster fixed to the roof.

"We'll walk from here," he said. "I think it will be safer."

The freighter that was moored under the walls of the Rajah's crumbling palace flew a five-starred flag that he recognized. It came from the People's Republic of China.

17

As they walked through the shadows, Durell heard the whine of winches, the chuffing of a donkey engine, and then the shout of a foreman, yelling in Cantonese to the laborers. The freighter, which wasn't more than 3000 tons, was off-loading crates and boxes in a sling, and the stuff was being piled up on a stone bulkhead to the rear of the Rajah's palace. Durell did not see anyone but the Chinese foreman in charge, but the man was anxious that none of the crates be given the slightest jar as they were being slung over the side and down on the dock.

"Does this go on often?" he asked softly.

Pala Mir shrugged. "It's just Paul's import-export business. Are you alarmed because the cargo comes from Red China? There is no restriction on trade with Peking here in Pasangara."

"What does your brother import?"

"I don't know. Gadgets. Consumer goods. Some radios, washing machines, things like that."

A stone pier intervened between the parked Land Rover and the palace. A tug was tied up to it but it rode without lights. Still, there could be a watchman on board, he decided. Beyond the moored tug was a crane, a black steel webbing against the sky, and then a row of sheds, some with thatched roofs and open on three sides, others with corrugated tin roofs and shut up tight. The shadows were very black between them.

Beyond the sheds was an open square planted with oleander shrubs that had grown up to giant size, a row of palms somewhat the worse for wear, and a drive that curved through the park to a monument that Durell saw was dimly carved in the royal shape of a turbaned man holding a staff of some sort in his left hand, while his right rested on the stone head of a Malay tiger.

"Anthony Merrydale?" he whispered to Pala Mir.

"The original," she said shortly.

"Are there watchmen?"

"There used to be a royal guard in the barracks over there. It's Paul's warehouse now."

He looked at the stone building against the Victorian fortress-palace. It was dark, some hundred yards from the dark where the Chinese ship was being unloaded.

He wondered what Hammond was doing at this moment.

"Come along," he said.

"I don't see why we have to arrive like thieves in the night. After all, the Rajah is expecting us. He sent for you, as I said."

He made no reply but moved quickly past the sheds, waiting for a moment to study the tug and the big waterfront crane. Then he stepped into the little park that adorned the facade of the stone palace. The old barracks were to the right, between him and the dock. He could hear the freighter's donkey engine and the winches, and they served to cover any noise he might make. The floodlights from the ship also cast a reflected glow behind the black bulk of the warehouse to let him see where he was going.

"The gate is the other way," Pala Mir said.

"I know. I'd like to look inside—unofficially."

The main doors facing what would be a truck lot were securely locked, but there were windows and a loading platform to the left, and from here he could see down the dock to the freighter tied up under the palace walls. He jumped up on the loading platform, flattened against the wall, and tried the door carefully. It was barred, but the hinges were loose, and he rocked them in and out for a moment, then shoved with his shoulder. It snapped open enough for him to squeeze through. Pala Mir was close on his heels.

He stopped short in the dusty darkness.

"Stand behind me," he told Pala Mir.

"What is it?"

"I don't know yet."

The warehouse door that had offered such easy access had already been forced by someone else. There were fresh splinters around the bar. Someone had left it that way, almost as if inviting him inside.

He took out his pencil flash and carefully examined the door and the floor around it, looking for trip wires and alarms, a booby trap of any kind. Everything looked normal except for the broken lock.

"What is it?" the girl asked again.

"We're a bit late."

The converted stone barracks was a cavernous place of dust and shadows, smelling of sisal, sawdust, and mildew. Part of it was built on piles over the water, and he heard an occasional splash of the tide under the teak floors.

Crates and cartons were piled up to the left and along the center of the floor, leaving two aisles on either side. He could not see over the stacked boxes.

He stood still and listened for a long time.

The shouts of the dockmen and the chuffing of the donkey engine wiped out all chance of hearing slight sounds. But it worked both ways, and he ventured to step away from the double doors after a moment. Pala Mir kept a light touch on his shoulder.

The labeling on most of the crates was Canadian or American—a dozen refrigerators, some air-conditioning units, a score of cartons containing cheap transistor radios. A new American car, a station wagon, gleamed in one corner. He was halfway down the first aisle, moving toward a dim glow of light that came through a window facing the dock when he stopped again.

He felt as if he were being lured into a trap.

Several of the radio boxes had been broken open to display their contents. The transistor sets inside looked innocent enough. He walked on a bit and then saw the man's legs protruding from between the two larger wooden boxes near the end of the aisle.

"Stay here, Pala Mir."

Her slight gasp betrayed the fact that she had seen it, too.

"Who is it?"

Durell shone the little flashlight into the crevice between the boxed merchandise. He saw Chiang Gi's white hair and brown face, the mouth open in surprise, the eyes blindly reflecting the light like black marbles.

The old fisherman's neck had been broken, neatly and expertly.

Durell pushed Pala Mir behind him and listened quietly for another long moment. He did not touch the dead man. He did not let himself think too much about it. He smelled the dust and oil in the warehouse, he heard the inner quietude under the muted noises from the dock, he felt sweat plaster his shirt to his back and shoulders.

"Oh, Sam. . . ."

"Somebody killed the old man. The killer may still be here."

"But who would want—he was such a dear man—"

He didn't reply. He moved quickly around the end of the stacked boxes to the opposite aisle. There was enough light here to do without his flashlight. It shone in from the floodlamps on the Chinese freighter nearby.

He thought he heard a sound. He froze, waited, and heard it again, then saw the small red eyes gleaming at him. Only a rat. He took another dozen steps and saw the open wooden crate, the small crowbar that had been used to force the seals, the gleam of printing on a carton inside.

The crate stood among a dozen others innocently labeled as auto engine parts. Outwardly, there was nothing to indicate why it had been chosen for burglary.

Durell studied the floor around it, risked his light beam again to check for hairline wires at throat height, but saw nothing dangerous. Pala Mir breathed lightly behind him.

One of the cartons inside the wooden crate had been broken open and another was revealed inside it. The inked stenciling read:

U.S. NAVY

Mk. 7 BMRG—7734

HANDLE WITH CARE

DELICATE INSTRUMENTS

Restricted

To Authorized Personnel

Only

XX47/88-70D

Durell said aloud: "Boomerangs! BMRG's. For the Judas planes. Some of the lot stolen in Saigon."

"I don't understand," Pala Mir whispered.

"Don't touch anything."

"But—"

He saw the note then.

It was a small scrap of paper tucked into the torn carton in such a way that he couldn't miss it. He studied the paper for a moment, checking its color and texture, to see if it might be Thermit-impregnated. It looked like an ordinary page torn from a notebook. It looked safe enough, he decided. Nothing was attached to it, but he removed it with extreme care, taking his time.

For a long time he studied the dark warehouse once more, listening, smelling, and sensing with every nerve. The place seemed empty. Pala Mir spoke impatiently, her voice suddenly fierce.

"Sam, I want to know who you are and how you knew something was wrong here in Paul's warehouse and why that poor old Chiang Gi was murdered. Was he a thief?"

"No."

"Did someone else break into this crate?"

"Yes."

He was thinking about the note. It was brief and unsigned: *"You're a bit late, Cajun. Sorry about Chiang."*

18

THE entrance to the old stone palace was on the opposite side of the dark park beyond the statue of the White Rajah, Anthony Merrydale, and his pet tiger. They were out of sight of the dock. Beyond the point of land was a row of dingy shops catering to fishermen and sailors. Most of the shops had signs over them in English and in East Indian. But the shops were all closed now and tightly shuttered.

The gates were formidable, built of solid teak, with a

chain leading up to a cluster of old iron bells. There was a small bridge leading up to it over a canal that made the spit of land and the building into an island. In addition, there was a heavy iron grill guarding the doors.

"Can we get in without sounding those bells?" Durell asked.

Pala Mir nodded in the dim light. Her dark Chinese clothing made her look slender and fragile, but he knew better. "Yes. One moment, please." She found a small push bell and put her thumb on it. "You must promise me something, Sam. I don't know too much about you, and yet I—I feel you can be my—my friend. If that's an understatement after last night on the sampan—well, you *did* save me from that mob last night, and I owe you more than I can repay. At the same time I must ask you, whatever you demand of me, not to disturb my grandfather."

"You said he wanted to see me."

"Yes, but please don't upset him. Don't tell him yet about Chiang Gi. The two old gentlemen knew each other very well and respected each other."

The heavy teak doors opened and the iron grill lifted automatically. A middle-aged Indian woman in a dark sari trimmed with silver looked out at them, her mouth wide and forbidding.

"Anandara, it is I, Pala Mir."

"Yes. You said you would come." The woman spoke in quiet, well-modulated English. "Is this the man?"

Pala Mir nodded and turned to Durell. "Anandara is my father's companion. No one else lives here."

"Where does your brother live?"

"Oh, he's in the city in one of the new apartments. He rarely comes here, except to badger Grandpapa."

They followed the Indian woman into a damp, vaulted corridor that smelled of must and mice with peeling ochre paint and a few Malay artifacts on the walls. One heavily framed portrait of the first Anthony Merrydale, haughtily arrogant and splendid in a jeweled turban and striped robes, stared down at them in the dim light. A flight of stairs led them quickly up out of this ground floor, which obviously was not used these days and perhaps had not been used for the last fifty years. The upper corridor was more pretentious but still gave evidence on the walls where paintings had been removed and presumably sold off.

He heard the faint sounds of the donkey engine and winches on the freighter through the thick stone walls. Pala Mir walked quickly, guided by the stately Anandara whose gray hair was pulled back into a heavy bun at the nape of her neck. They turned right, then paused before an ornate, gold-leafed double door. On the walls to either side were Malay spears and kris and a collection of military rifles.

Pala Mir said, "Sam, I suppose you think I am vicious and dissolute, as the newspapers said, and my brother a paragon of virtue. Everyone says so, so it must be true. And yet—"

"I know you better now," he told her.

"No, you do not know me. Nor have you met my dear grandfather." She hesitated, with distress in her slightly slanted, Eurasian eyes. She resembled a wounded doe. "I told you, Grandpapa is a bit strange. Is it true that your own grandfather lived in the past, too?"

"He stopped the clock for himself in defense against a grief too heavy to bear," said Durell.

"And you understand this? You love him?"

"I do, and I regard him as one of the finest men I've been privileged to know."

She bit her lip. "It is the same with the Rajah, you know. But he is not insane or senile, as Paul tries to prove!" Her voice lifted in stifled anger, while Anandara just stood to one side, silent and impassive. "Oh, I get so furious with my own twin brother! He charges Grandpapa with wanting to turn back the clock and rule Pasangara again, but it is not so! Grandpapa is loyal to the new state and the new democracy. You must believe that. It is just that he remembers the past glory and power of the Merrydales here, and he prefers to pretend sometimes that the past still exists, because of today's ugly and inglorious present. Is that such a terrible thing?"

"If he's happy, it's wonderful."

Pala Mir nodded. "Then come, Sam, meet my grandfather, the last White Rajah of Pasangara."

She pushed open the great double-leafed doors.

He stepped back in time into all the mysterious pomp and splendor of Malaya's power of the last century. In this great chamber, overlooking the sea through narrow, slotted windows, everything had been preserved as it had been in the days of the first Rajah. The first Anthony Merrydale may have been a pirate on an international scale, but his taste in art had been impeccable. Buddhist carvings, sculptures large and small taken from inland temples, adorned the walls. There were ivories, mounted elephant tusks, tiger skins, polished Arab weapons, intricate woven patterns of plaited stuff, gold Indian plaques, and Chinese jade and porcelain. The room had a raised floor at the window end with three wide, carpeted stairs going up, embellished with an astrolabe, an ivory screen, and dim Victorian paintings the worse for wear in this tropical climate. The interior stone walls had been imported from England, Durell guessed, for griffins and stone monsters leered and menaced any intruder from the corners.

But it was the old man, seated on a tiger-skin throne with an umbrella-like silk canopy above it, that caught Durell's immediate attention.

Despite the sullen heat of the night, the White Rajah wore a massive cloak of silk, a white turban with a white plume sprouting from a huge yellow gem above the forehead, and ornate rings on skeletal fingers. His silvery hair, peering from under the regal turban, was cut long in thin white strands. The old man's nose was long and strong, the mouth cruel as only that of an adventurer, seizing power and royal authority in distant lands by sheer force of personality, had to be cruel. The face was static, but its serenity was belied by the eyes.

The eyes were neither senile nor addled. They were

sharp and intelligent, even amused, hospitable but remotely polite.

"Ah," the old man said in Oxonian English. "The American who was so helpful to my beloved granddaughter. We welcome you, sir. Did you know, my dear fellow, that once when temple bells rang throughout Pasangara and the priests chanted for Buddha's wisdom and blessings, the response of the worshippers was, 'To the Serene and Excellent Rajah, health and honor, long life and perpetual victory'?"

"Grandpapa—" Pala Mir murmured.

"Have no fears, child. I do not demand such salutations in these days." The old man smiled at Durell's tall figure. Somehow, despite the theatrical getup, he did not seem ridiculous at all. "I must say, sir, that rather than mistake you for another of those bustling American businessmen or political bureaucrats, I would take you for one of my father's great mercenary captains, who carved this province out of hostile jungle and subdued the local tribes to bend them to his will and civilize them."

"Grandpapa—" the girl warned again.

The Indian woman said gently, "Let him speak, my dear."

"I amuse myself, Pala Mir." Again those shrewd eyes, as ancient as his royal Oriental costume, bored right through Durell. "Yes, my dear fellow, there is something fearful about you. Once, of course, there was true splendor in this court—riches and honors and good works for the people of Pasangara. Exploitation, yes, and tyranny, too—even terror when necessary. The White Rajah employed several mercenaries like you, Mr. Durell. There is that air about you, yes, of danger and cold death."

"Mr. Merrydale—" Durell began.

The old man held up a hand; rings glittered on his thin fingers. "Permit me, sir. I know men. Once, you would have been the right hand of the Rajah, the man to send villains and traitors to be strangled for betraying the state. Who then was immune from the Rajah's eyes? I believe, my dear sir, that my palace has been invaded by you, in a sense, and perhaps I shall wind up as a corpse floating in the coastal swamps."

"I assure you, I am from the twentieth century," said Durell.

"But you are a rajah's man. I see it, I see it!" the old gentleman said triumphantly. "Do you dispute your true vocation?"

Pala Mir spoke gently. "Grandpapa, Mr. Durell has been helpful to me, and he is a friend who needs help in return. He wants your permission to visit the mountain palace." She turned her grave, dark-blue eyes to Durell. "Is that not so?"

"Yes. If I could—"

"And what of the civil and military authorities, eh?" The old man cackled and wobbled his head; his great turban jewels flashed and sparkled. "Well, never mind, never mind. I am still respected here. And I understand you, sir. I fear you but I like you."

The White Rajah stood up from his throne and proved taller and stronger than Durell had expected. His long silk gown fell away in enormous pleats, revealing stupendous striped pantaloons and leather slippers with curled, pointed toes. "You are welcome here and welcome to my aid. It is not often now that I am consulted. I understand the state is in danger, and whatever honors have been stripped from me, I am loyal and devoted to the welfare of Pasangara."

"I assure you, I have no intention of meddling in the security of the province."

"Perhaps not. We shall see. Once, of course, when I was rich, my poor Pala Mir would have wanted for nothing, and she would have been a happy child—"

"I want nothing now, Grandpapa."

"I know, my dear. Well, well. I am consulted at last." The Rajah was pleased. He looked cunningly at Durell. "There are saboteurs, guerrillas, Red agents in the mountains, did you know that? My poor country has been the object of invasion since history began, my dear Durell. From Kubla Khan, who sent naval expeditions to the

Malayan independent kingdoms, on through the Portuguese Admiral Lopez de Sequeira, who brought letters from the king of Portugal to the great Sultan Mahmud. Do you know our true history, sir, and our longing for freedom? Do you know the fine stories of our national heroes Tun Perak, the Kingmaker, and Hang Tuah, the Malay admiral? We have not always been cursed by guns, of course. The Apostle of the Indies, Francis Xavier, once visited Pasangara, too. We have been shuttled back and forth between the Dutch, the Portuguese, the British, the English East India Company, and the Dutch United Company for generations. We have had civil wars between Malay chieftains, Chinese tin miners, and British rubber planters for much too long."

"Grandpapa—" Pala Mir said again.

"Permit me, child. One must keep matters in proper perspective. We have Indian workers on the rubber estates, Chinese in the tin mines, Malays in the rural villages. Everyone has been tolerated and welcomed in a spirit of peace and unity. Malaya has much to be proud of. We fought the Chinese Communist agents after the Second World War, we resettled our refugees in the 'new villages,' and ultimately we defeated those guerrillas in their jungle hideouts."

The old man seemed to achieve a new height and dignity as he spoke. "Now we are in difficulty again from those who will not let us live in peace. The city and the countryside are dangerous. My hands are tied, of course." The Rajah shrugged. "I am still suspect in our new democracy. I do not mind. I would give all I have, or hope to have, to help, and if I could go back to the mountain palace, I would be rich again and perhaps be of some use—"

Pala Mir said, "Grandpapa insists there are chests of gold coins there, hidden by the first Rajah."

"No, no, nothing so romantic as hidden treasure, my child. Simply a precaution taken by my father for extra funds in time of emergency. Nobody believes me. Paul thinks my wits are addled when I speak of it. But if you would help me, Mr. Durell," his eyes grew sly but amused, "I would go with you for whatever purposes you have there. I would pay you well—"

"No need for that," Durell said.

"We will arrange it, then. At once. No time like the present, eh? Is the city safe now? Have the riots ended? Colonel Tileong was here this afternoon to impress upon me the necessity of staying in the palace, in view of the temper of my poor children, my poor Malays who suffer and are so patient—"

The Rajah paused suddenly, and Durell saw the moldering curtains at the window flutter slightly in a warm draft. He knew the doors to the enormous room had been opened behind him, and he turned casually but not before he saw the incredible change come over the gallant old man.

Where there had been strength and a cynical amusement, there was now a look of blank vapidity, of childish guilt. A vacuous expression now appeared in the suddenly faded eyes. The long nose drooped. The jeweled turban looked foolish. A trembling finger came up a corner of the mouth and clung to the lower lip, moving a bead of saliva on it.

"Paul, dear boy?"

Durell saw Pala Mir's twin brother in the doorway. The Indian woman, Anandara, made a small gesture, her hand rising to her full bosom; she seemed to shrink a little in her silver-trimmed sari.

"Grandpapa," said Paul Merrydale, "I warned you not to have anything to do with this man. Why did you disobey me?"

"Dear boy, I—I'm sorry—"

"Let the Rajah be," said Anandara quietly.

"Shut up," Paul snapped. "I've had about enough of your orders, too, ever since I was a boy. Things have changed in Pasangara, haven't you heard?" He swung around to Durell. "As for you, your days here are ended, understand?"

Paul Merrydale was not alone. Two Chinese stood behind him. One wore a maritime officer's cap and obviously came from the freighter—a burly man from Szechwan with a sharp nose and intelligent, hostile eyes. The other Chinese was a seaman who swung a heavy billy club from a thong wrapped around his wrist.

Paul was as elegant as ever in a white drill suit and a flowered cravat. Whatever the hour—and it was past midnight now—he seemed to have just stepped from a bandbox. His elegance, however, was deceptive.

"Grandpapa—"

The old Rajah made a quavering sound of fear "Grandson, you must protect me! I am an old man, and I am not political, as you know."

"Exactly. You and Pala have been foolish enough. Please do not interfere now."

"Of course not, Paul. Do as you think best."

Merrydale fixed his pale eyes on Durell. "You will stay here until the police come."

Before Durell could reply, the telephone rang.

The sound was incongruous in that barbaric, splendid room. Durell had not seen the instrument, but Paul Merrydale knew where it was. He moved with a long stride and pushed aside a bronze-studded Malay shield and took the phone from the wall. He spoke angrily. "The Palace. What is it?"

There was an awkward pause. The two Chinese from the freighter blocked the exit. Their slanted eyes never left Durell's tall figure. Durell stood quietly while Merrydale listened to someone explosive on the telephone. Then Paul said angrily, "It is no concern of yours. He is not in *my* custody. Perhaps you should speak to Colonel Tileong."

Again there was a pause, and then Merrydale turned impatiently and thrust the telephone at Durell.

"Mr. Condon, your consul, wants to speak to you."

"Thank you."

David Condon's voice was high and light, quick and

urgent. "Durell? I know you can't talk. I took a chance hoping you'd be there. Are you all right?"

"For the moment," Durell said quietly.

"Threatened?"

"Yes."

"Chinese?"

"And Merrydale, Junior."

Paul Merrydale bit his lip. Durell stared at him with blank eyes while he listened to the young diplomat speak with a rush of words into the earphone.

"That's not the worst of it. You got out only because I finally figured where you were and got Premier Kuang on an urgent diplomatic protest concerning you. But you seem to have a penchant for trouble. I really shouldn't be involved with you at all; I have my own directives, as you know—"

"We want the same thing," Durell said.

"Yes. Well. Be that as it may, Tileong is on his way to the Rajah now—after you, of course."

"Why?"

"He's had a tip, apparently. The premier made a small mention of it just minutes ago. You'd better get out of there."

"Why?" Durell asked again, insistent.

"It seems that someone—Tileong thinks it was George Hammond—says you are responsible for Chiang Gi's death. Anonymous tip. I don't know anything more about it. I want to see you at once before Tileong takes you again and we build a nasty incident out of it."

"Don't clutch," Durell said.

"Well, it looks as if Hammond, for some reason, wants you on ice for a while. I've run a nice quiet ship here, and, thanks to that, the authorities have been willing to cooperate with me." Condon's voice was young and self-important again. "Just the same, I'd rather see you out of Pasangara as soon as possible."

"I'm on my way," Durell said.

He hung up.

Merrydale had been listening, but Durell did not think

he could have made too much out of the one-sided conversation he'd heard. Durell ignored him and walked over to the White Rajah on his dilapidated, mildewed throne. He shook the old man's left hand; the Rajah's right hand still groped childishly in his mouth. He bowed to Pala Mir, looked at Paul Merrydale, and said, "You will have to excuse me. A diplomatic conference with Premier Kuang, I'm afraid. Do you have any objections if I leave?"

Merrydale's eyes glittered with a moment's passing rage, "Anandara, show him out."

The Hindu woman nodded and glided silently to the huge double doors, her sari floating like a cloud around her body. Durell followed her down the stairs and along the moldy corridor that led to the front gates of the palace. He thought he heard a distant siren whine, but he wasn't sure.

The Indian woman looked at him with liquid eyes.

"Be at the Chungsu Bridge at dawn this morning. At five o'clock," she said quietly.

"Thank you."

"I thank *you* for being kind to my young mistress."

"How did she get the message to you?"

Anandara merely smiled as she showed him out.

19

HE walked alone along the waterfront. The night was suddenly very dark, very empty. The humidity was a burden with every breath he took. The stars reeled overhead. He was aware of a bone-deep tiredness and wanted noth-

ing more than to return to the Kuan Diop Hotel to sleep.
But that would mean disaster. No place was safe in this
tense, silent city. Wondering where Hammond might be,
he searched the shadows automatically, feeling a deep sor-
row for Chiang Gi whose body lay in the warehouse, and
then dismissed the emotion as dangerous and distracting.

Every dark corner held a potential enemy.

He saw a launch approach the dock where the Chinese
freighter was tied up and thought he recognized Tileong's
dapper little figure in the bow. He walked on. Not even
Pala Mir's Land Rover was safe, at the moment. He
turned into an alley, walked past some thatch-roofed warehouses, came to a row of tiny Indian shops, turned another corner, and came back to the waterfront esplanade
behind the Rover. It was only a darker bulk against the
bulk of the shed where he had parked it.

He saw no movement there.

He waited a minute, another minute, gave it five. He
did not move. The vehicle looked innocent enough. Nobody seemed to be waiting in ambush there. He heard a
siren. Then a local Army car rolled by, but he did not
stir and was not seen.

He thought he smelled cigar smoke above the pungent,
aromatic waterfront smells.

He waited.

There was a glint of reflection from the side of the
Land Rover, a fleck of starlight on the windshield. It
moved slightly, winked out, then shone again.

He smelled the cigar smoke once more.

He looked behind him, suddenly expecting to be bush-
whacked. Colonel Tileong and his men had hurried into
the palace; Durell kept his attention on the car.

At last he could clearly define the shadow of the man
who waited there for him.

He had no intention of keeping a date with death.

Turning, he walked quietly away.

He slept for three hours in a shed not too distant from
the palace, open to the waterfront. There were huge piles

of sisal bags that were redolent of spices and urine. A bicycle leaned against one wall of the shed, carelessly chained to a post. Durell made himself comfortable in a black corner where he could see the harbor, and after about twenty minutes, he heard the motor of the Rover start up about a hundred yards away from him. It moved slowly, searchingly, down the wide street facing the wharves, and then the sound of its engine faded.

After that, he went to sleep.

At ten minutes before five he awoke, aware of stiffness all through his body, with aches in particular areas that Lieutenant Parepa had favored. The bridge of his nose was tender, and he could still feel Parepa's knuckles on it. His left eye was slightly swollen. On the whole, however, he felt better.

He borrowed the loose bicycle in the shed and peddled slowly down the wide street toward the Chungsu bridge. Pasangara was quiet. For a change, there were no red fires glowing in the sky from the Chinese quarter.

Dawn was only fifteen minutes away. There was already a faint lightening over the horizon of the South China Sea. A light winked green and then red at the end of the harbor breakwater. He heard the throb of marine engines, then saw the Chinese freighter slowly make its way toward the open sea.

Coming out of alleys and byways, other bicycles made their appearance on the streets, the men and women in wide, conical straw hats, the women like birds in their bright sarongs and occasional European skirts. The men wore white or black. A traffic policeman stood on a pedestal at one end of the Chungsu bridge and yawned at the colors in the eastern sky. Durell noted some food stalls opening along the side streets; his hunger was aroused. Then he passed a European-style café whose Chinese proprietor was just taking down the shutters. Several whites—Dutchmen, he gathered from the low scatter of their voices as he peddled by—were taking tables on the sidewalk. A few pedicabs made their appearance.

Pasangara seemed ready to return to normal.

The sign over the café read "Segun Maj" and the smell of coffee increased his hunger. From the sidewalk he could watch the Chungsu bridge well enough, and he turned the bicycle in the growing traffic, aware of a fresh, cool breeze blowing from over the reaches of the river mouth.

Nobody paid attention to him as he chose a table and ordered a European breakfast of coffee, rolls, and eggs. The overseas Chinese proprietor was adept at catering to Western tastes. One of the Dutchmen nearby, lifting his round head, stared at Durell and made a tentative gesture with his hand, but Durell got up and bought a packet of Indian cigarettes, so the man turned back to his companions. A small boy delivered a paper-wrapped box, put it on the zinc counter just inside the doorway, then peddled away.

Ten minutes later Durell saw the Land Rover.

Pala Mir was driving. Her grandfather sat regally beside her on the front seat.

He got up and ignored his bicycle in the rack and crossed the street. Pala Mir saw him and waved.

Then something struck him in the back. He staggered forward, feeling a gush of heat, and then heard the ear-splitting roar of an explosion behind him.

He saw Pala Mir's face, white and shocked, and then he threw himself flat in the street as debris from the shattered café slapped and crashed down around him.

Smoke and flame gushed from the café entrance. Where the Dutchmen had been sitting at their breakfast, there was only an insane tangle of wreckage and scattered blobs of flesh, a torn limb twitching by itself. He remembered the delivery boy on the bicycle and the packet left in the café entrance under the sign that read "Segun Maj." The sign was gone, the chairs blown to bits, the tables strewn in the street around him.

Pala Mir waved him on anxiously.

Durell got up and walked quickly to her car, while

the other pedestrians and pedicabs in the dawn-lighted street stood in shocked disbelief, looking at the terrorist disaster.

20

No one paid attention to them or tried to stop them as they drove through the tide of running people on the Chungsu Bridge. The sound of a woman's screams and the wail of a siren touched them briefly. At the end of the bridge Pala Mir raced the Land Rover down the riverside road.

"Go slow," Durell warned. "Otherwise, they'll think we did it."

She slowed to a normal speed in the city streets, turned off the esplanade, and took a long detour around the Kuan Diop Hotel. The river steamer was gone from its dock.

Durell turned to look at the Rajah. All traces of the old man's brief spasm of senility, when Paul had confronted him last night, were erased. His eyes were clear and even twinkling with amusement.

"Good morning, sir," the Rajah said.

He wore a bush jacket with huge pockets and a heavy revolver in a belt around his waist. His legs were encased in strong, polished boots. He said, "I have some appropriate clothing for you, too, Mr. Durell."

"Are we going to your mountain palace?"

"Isn't that where you wished to go?"

"Yes. Doesn't Paul object?"

"Paul knows nothing about it. I am a loyal citizen of Pasangara, my dear sir, and the past is the past. Pasangara belongs to the future, and I will not be idle while that future is destroyed. I have the feeling that your duties in Pasangara coincide with the best interests of the state."

"It does, I assure you," Durell said.

Wearing a khaki shirt, riding pants, and boots, Pala Mir looked freshly groomed in the morning light. She, too, was armed. She drove competently, and in a few minutes they came out on a graveled riverside road that soon became a tunnel through the jungle. It was growing hot.

"Did the police find Chiang Gi?" Durell asked.

"Yes. They were tipped off, so they knew exactly where to look. Paul was in a fury. He was questioned by Tileong, but you're the principal suspect." Her eyes twinkled. "You seem to have spent an uncomfortable night."

"Not bad. Have the Pao Thets been active in terrorist bombings like this morning?"

"It's their boldest effort yet," she said.

Now and then through the jungle, they noticed the sluggish, serpentine reaches of the Pasangara River. The heat built up rapidly. They stopped once for Durell to change into a bush shirt and boots that the Rajah provided. There were Thermos bottles of water, a kit of food, boxes of ammunition, and two Uzi automatic rifles made in Israel, the Uzi being one of the handiest weapons recently developed. Durell kept one on his lap as Pala Mir continued to drive.

By the river bank they passed two villages on stilts, and their passage attracted little interest. Among the rice paddies of the countryside things seemed normal.

Pala Mir spoke calmly about her brother and about her growing suspicion that the mountain palace and plantation were being used as a base by the Pao Thets to disturb the peace of the countryside. The Rajah dozed in his seat, although the road became primitive beyond the second village, thus causing the Land Rover to jounce painfully. Durell watched the jungle. The sun was well up, and the air was like the breath of a hot oven. Parrots, monkeys, and once a small cheetah-like cat appeared in the trees. They came to a sharp bend and then a pontoon bridge over the river, and when Pala Mir started to cross, Durell checked her.

"Wait. Stop the car."

She did as he asked. "What is it?"

"Back up into the shadow, please."

"I don't see anything."

He pointed to the muddy river bank where the road ran down out of the jungle to the plank bridge. Several sets of new tire tracks looked freshly printed in the mud.

"Did you see Tileong before you left the palace this morning?"

"No, he was long gone, by then."

"And your brother?"

The Rajah said, "Paul went to his apartment, quite angry with me for tolerating my dear Pala Mir."

Durell shut off the motor. "Let's wait a bit."

"But it's a long way, possibly a night of travel, to get to the plantation," Pala Mir objected.

The old Rajah chuckled. "Listen to Mr. Durell, child. When I said he was a mercenary and a man to be feared, I was sincere. Do you see them, Mr. Durell?"

Durell nodded. Across the width of the river, which should have been dotted with Malay fishing boats, the opposite bank looked green, empty, forbidding. Beyond it was the distant loom of the interior hills, vague in the jungle's heat haze. There was a small village of thatched huts on poles to the left of the bridge on the far side, but not a soul was in sight.

"Look to the left," Durell said. "Near the village. Two degrees off the south end of the bridge."

Something glinted there. A ribbon of pale color suddenly moved against the dense green. Then another glint.

The Rajah chuckled again. "Rifles, Mr. Durell?"

"Yes. But who are they?"

"Pao Thets, perhaps."

"Or Tileong's militia, waiting for us."

"Perhaps."

"Is there another road we can use?"

"No." Pala Mir looked distressed. "If we can't cross here, we're stopped before we've hardly started."

"Not at all, child," said the Rajah. "There is another road, quite old, perhaps forgotten. Back up, Durell, as if we are turning back. It may deceive those people."

Durell took the wheel from the girl and retreated a quarter of a mile down the river to where a narrow jungle trail forked to the left. It soon became a fairly well-defined route through the jungle vines.

"This is an old hunting trail cut originally by my father," said the old man. "It can take us a bit farther. There is a shallow ford about fifteen miles southwest of here. The main channel divides before that, so the river steamer can reach the old plantation station at Trang Bhatu. The town fell on bad times during the old Red warfare in the '50s—destroyed the rubber farms. But I think the way will be safe."

Durell did not agree but he kept silent.

No one had used this road before them. The vines that had overgrown the trail were intact, and their progress was slow and tedious. Durell had to get out again and again to chop away the creepers that blocked the way. It was hot, savage work. The old man offered to help with a machete, but his vitality ebbed as the jungle heat built up. Their progress almost came to a halt. The river was lost to sight. At eleven o'clock they stopped to drink cold tea and eat the sandwiches Pala Mir had prepared.

"I have enough food for three days," she said quietly. "Enough to get us there and back."

"Does Paul ever go to the plantation?"

"Now and then he flies up there. He has his own plane. A Beechcraft."

"There's an airstrip up in the hills?"

"Oh, yes. Paul built it long ago."

There had been no airstrip marked on the charts Durell had studied. At noon they saw the river again.

The road improved, joining another that followed the river bank. The stream was still deep enough for the steamer from Pasangara. The jungle was silent, the river empty of boats. A telephone line that presumably went down to the capital was cut, the wires hanging limply from canted poles. The first straggling houses of the town were empty. A few chickens pecked at the dust. A pig squealed; dogs barked and howled. A naked child playing in the middle of the road looked at them with bewildered eyes.

"Where is everyone?" Pala Mir asked.

They found the first dead man in the middle of the road to the steamer dock. He was a Malay, wearing a cloth headband and a colorful skirt that was too wet and too red. His throat was cut and he had been mutilated. He had not been dead for very long.

There was a smell of charred wood, smoke, and death. A government inn stood on the waterfront with the door blown in and half the wall crumbled by a grenade or mortar shell. Durell stopped the Land Rover in the shade of a tree beside the inn and surveyed the small town square on the river's edge.

There was only the blinding sun, the silence, and the smell of destruction. Trang Bhatu, despite its gloss of modern improvements, still reflected the age of the Golden Peninsula known to Vasco da Gama, Sir Francis Drake, and the early Portuguese and Dutch explorers. Malacca, he reflected, was once the rich land of rubber and tin, a crucible of race and culture from all of Southeast Asia. Ancient Cathay and Hindu had blended with the old Malay pomp, warmth, and pageantry. Once a languorous village, Trang Bhatu had grown with the river and road traffic, but there were still Arab shops, a few die-hard Dutch and Javanese left by the high tide of centuries-old piracy, plunder, and trade.

Durell took his Uzi and walked past a shop that exhibited Chinese magazines, Malay *bajus,* white Indian cotton *dhotis,* and *salwa-kamiz.* He paused at the blown-in entrance to the inn. There was an old photograph of the

Tengku, of the Kedah royal family, in one window. Japanese transistor radios sat side by side with beautifully carved ivory and teak bowls. There had been no looting.

He paused again. The government flag had been torn from its staff. There were crates and bales on the dock, waiting for the steamer that had never gotten here today. Across the little park on the river's edge was a small Mosque, cheek by jowl with a Buddhist temple. Religion was no problem in Malaya. Islam, Christianity, Hinduism, Sikhism, and Taoism earned the respect and tolerance of their neighbors.

But there had been little tolerance of human life in Trang Bhatu this morning.

He kept the Uzi ready.

Pala Mir started out of the Rover, and he waved her back to safety. Dust moved in a hot wind that blew across the river. He flattened against the wall beside the shattered door of the inn and heard only the scratching of a chicken in the dust. Several bicycles lay on their sides in the square under a massive banyan tree. Sunlight twinkled through the leaves. The chicken walked into the doorway, clucking slightly.

Durell moved in fast, the Uzi cocked. The shadows inside were thick with dust and a smell of sweat. A Malay clerk was at the desk to his right, head resting on his folded forearm; he had been shot in the back of the neck.

Squatting on the floor in a corner, a thin woman in a torn sarong rocked back and forth, staring at him with unseeing eyes. She was the first living human being he had come upon.

A scrap of paper was pinned to her breast.

Durell stared at her across the hot shadows and she stared back. He listened to the chicken moving around in the back room. After a moment he walked over to the woman and read the note: *"If you've gotten to this place, Cajun, you've come too far."*

Durell spoke quietly to Pala Mir. "Hammond is ahead of us. He's determined to reach your grandfather's mountain palace first, and he'll do anything to stop me from getting there before he makes it."

She frowned. "But I thought you worked with him."

"I did. But he has a devil on his back."

"Did he try to kill you last night?"

"I think so."

"Would he try again?"

"Perhaps. He's not quite sane now. I know all about it, and I'm sorry for him, but that doesn't make him any less dangerous."

The Rajah said, "It is distressing. It would be difficult enough to cope with the Pao Thets, who have become much bolder since the city riots. Or with Tileong, who has tagged you as a criminal, sir. Or even to overcome the obstructions of my erring grandson, who is obsessed with hatred for you. But to have your own compatriot in a kind of devil's footrace against you—"

Durell nodded. He didn't like the feeling of the ruined, empty town. "Could you speak in Malay to a woman in there, sir? She's in shock but it might help."

The tall old man got out of the Land Rover with slow dignity. His white hair gleamed in the sunlight. The stunned woman still rocked on her haunches in the corner of the shattered inn. The chicken pecked about her naked feet. Her toenails had been painted.

"Ask if she's heard any planes go over lately. Jets. Lots of noise. Coming down."

The old man frowned. "I don't understand—"

The woman stared at Durell's Uzi, and she was mute until he put it aside and smiled at her. The Rajah spoke gently but with an air of paternal authority. It was doubtful if she recognized him as the former ruler of the province. She simply moaned and rocked from side to side as the Rajah put the question to her. Then she muttered, closed her eyes, and nodded.

"She says yes, several times," the Rajah repeated.

"How many times?"

"She is not sure. Almost two hands, she says."

"Between five and ten times, then. Ask her if they all went the same way."

The Rajah's quiet voice lulled the frightened woman. She nodded again. "Now ask her," Durell said, "who destroyed the village. Then describe George Hammond, and ask if she has seen him this morning."

The soft Malay words went back and forth in the dusty sunlight. The Rajah said, "She is not sure who the men were who shot up Trang Bhatu. They came at dawn. She remembers the Communist terror in the rubber plantations twenty years ago, and she says it was like that but worse, more brutal. They killed her husband. As for George Hammond—yes, she says a man like that was here shortly after the Pao Thets."

"Alone?"

"Yes."

"Is he still in the village?"

The Rajah asked the question, then shrugged. "She does not know. He was here less than an hour ago."

The river ran wide and shallow at the ford above the town. Fallen trees and debris, swept down from the hills, made a natural dam, a vast tangle of logs, stones, and tangled brush. Sunlight twinkled on the sand and the mud shallows below it. Hunting small fish in the pools formed by the low water, long-legged birds moved as if on stilts. Durell stopped the car at the river's edge and surveyed the opposite bank with the Rajah's field glasses.

The low-growing jungle seemed empty of all life. He scanned it for several moments before he nodded.

"Let's go."

21

Two miles beyond the ford the primitive road joined the main highway to the mountains. They passed through small, empty villages, but none had been destroyed like Trang Bhatu. Merrydale explained that the highway had been built for expressway buses to the inland mountain resorts, but there was no traffic on the road now.

Gradually, the land lifted above the miasmic coastal swamps, but clouds formed, coming in from the South China Sea, and presently it began to rain in huge, warm drops, that soon developed into a torrential downpour.

At two in the afternoon Durell caught a glint of something shiny in the rear mirror. The road had narrowed, and after a curve lifted to the right through a gorge, he caught another glimmer of the light. He waited five minutes, and then he was certain. He began looking for a place to pull off the highway. The jungle was close by on every hand. For the past half hour they had seen no villages, but there were terraced rice paddies and incurious farmers in conical straw hats, working plows behind their water buffalo. The Rover shook the planks of a small bridge. Then they came upon some fields where two naked boys astride a buffalo waved and rapped the great horned beast with their wands.

"Are we being followed?" the Rajah asked quietly.

Durell thought the old gentleman had grown in strength and stature since they had started. The few people they had passed in the fields had recognized him, and one man had shouted and waved. Durell looked in the mirror again.

"Motorcycles and a troop-carrying truck."

"Can we outrun them?"

"I doubt it."

"If you don't mind a suggestion, my dear chap——"

"It would be welcome," Durell said dryly.

"Good. You are in command here. But I do know the country, sir. It was once *my* country, in a sense. We must turn off about two miles farther on, anyway. There's an old rubber farm there—MacCampbell had it, a fine lad, but the Communists got him in '51, or was it '50? Never mind. It's been abandoned for years. We could pull off there and see if the military turn off after us. If they do, they're on the way to the mountains, too."

"Would it be Colonel Tileong?"

"No doubt of it. A most capable and energetic gentleman. He helped organize the Kota Tinggi Jungle Warfare School with the British, refining jungle fighting techniques learned against the Red insurgents in our emergency of the 1950s. The Thais and the South Vietnamese have sent officers here to learn how we won our struggle then."

"Tell me," Durell said, "are you afraid of Paul?"

The Rajah cleared his throat. "Well, about my grandson. . . The past is over with and best forgotten. My title is an anachronism today. I put on quite a show for you last night, I fear. As for Paul, he insists I am senile, and he terrifies me, frankly. I cannot control him now. He is anxious to dominate Pasangara's affairs. He actually considered running against Premier Kuang in the last election—and got soundly trounced, of course. Upset him dreadfully. Hasn't been the same since."

"Why are you afraid of him?"

The old man said, "Because Paul is dangerous, sir."

"How? To whom?"

"He is too ambitious. He works day and night at his business; he is possessed by a drive to succeed. He has shown some jealousy toward my dear Pala——"

Pala Mir, in the back of the Rover, interrupted, "We'd better turn off soon. The military is in a hurry."

The road was a desolate path through gloomy rows of rubber trees that the jungle had hastened to repossess long ago. The rain persisted. After a half mile the Rajah gestured to the right, and Durell turned the jouncing vehicle into an even smaller trail that led deeper into the gray shadows. He cut the ignition. They sat and listened. Soon they heard the growing beat of motorcycles and truck engines through the pattering rain; the echoes reverberated along the dark rows of abandoned trees. Then the sounds died away.

"Good," said the old man. "They are taking the main road to my former estate. We can reach the mountains quicker this way through MacCampbell's place."

Durell moved to the ignition key, then halted. A new sound came through the waves of soughing wind and rain. Low-hanging clouds seemed to touch the tops of the towering rubber trees. He looked up, but the vines and bamboo that had penetrated this once-cultivated area blocked off the sky.

But that sound was unmistakable. It was a small, twin-prop plane, flying low and to the southwest.

The Rajah made a small sound of annoyance. "I'm afraid that is Paul's private aircraft. Pala Mir has flown in it several times, is that correct, my dear?"

The girl nodded and Durell said, "He's heading for the mountain palace."

The old man nodded grimly. "I do wish you would explain your objective, Mr. Durell. Everyone seems to have a purpose in suddenly making for the mountains, but I am still in the dark. Very few people from Pasangara come this way since the Pao Thet disturbances began."

Durell started the engine and headed deeper into the abandoned plantation. The trail was rough but not impossible. The rain was heavier. There was a sharp-angled turn to the right, then a climbing slope that made the car pitch and groan. After a mile they came out on a cleared area of low-growing brush. A deserted village of workers' huts appeared out of the gloom. It had been empty a long time, and the houses were overgrown with vines. Just beyond it on a knoll stood a long, low house of mahogany boarding with a wide porch. Fire had eaten away one end of the building, but most of it still stood. Bamboo grew up around it, forty feet tall, making a dense growth that screened them from the house. Halfway there, a fallen log barred the way. Durell braked and listened to the rain and wind in the mabolo.

"Stay here," he said.

"Let me help you move the log," said the Rajah.

"Better not."

Durell walked carefully up the trail to the fallen tree. He carried the Uzi with him. Rain quickly soaked him. As he studied the trail, his face grew grim. He took two more cautious steps and halted. He heard the Rajah get out of the car behind him, but he did not look around.

He took another step, then saw the drangh trap—almost too late.

There was a sharp snapping sound, a whir, a violent thrashing, and then three bamboo javelins hissed through the air. He had only a split second to throw himself sidewise and flat.

There was a metallic clang as one of the spears hit the Land Rover. Pala Mir screamed, and Durell rolled into the thick bamboo beside the path. There came a second snapping sound, and the drangh released three more of the needle-point bamboo lances. They whirred overhead and fell harmlessly beyond the vehicle.

Durell got slowly to his feet. The old Rajah stood beside the Rover, his face pale with anger.

"It was a favorite booby trap of the Communists," the old man said. "Back in '52, one of my best friends was killed this way."

"Are you all right?" Durell asked.

"Yes, thanks."

"Pala Mir?"

"Yes," she said.

The trap was made by carefully concealed trip wires in the rubble of the trail, connected to bent poles that released the triple shafts under great tension. Durell walked carefully around the fallen log and saw that it had been chopped down only recently. The wood was fresh and clean. Anger filled him as he heaved the roadblock out of the way.

"Let's go."

The Rover became useless just below the plantation house. There was a deep gorge and a wooden bridge, and the banks over the rushing stream were dense with more bamboo. The house was clearly visible only a few hundred yards away with the trail distinctly outlined beyond it but vanishing into the jungle toward the misty hills. The rain hissed, poured, then streamed down with a suddenly heavier intensity.

"More trouble," Durell said.

"The bridge?" asked the Rajah.

"It's another trap. Get out of the car. Take the weapons and water. How far is it to your palace?"

"From here, perhaps ten miles, all uphill."

Durell studied the tall, gaunt old man. "Can you make it?"

"I believe so. I am not entirely decrepit."

There came a faint shout just then from the opposite side of the gorge. For a moment Durell saw nothing. Then the cry was repeated, and he heard a dim crashing in the brush. A girl came running toward the bridge.

It was Lily Fan.

"Durell!" she cried. "Help me!"

The Rajah started forward, but Durell put a hand on his arm. "Wait."

Lily Fan came to a halt just at the opposite end of the small bridge. The bridge was built of planks and timbers, and although long out of use and vine-grown, it looked solid enough. The girl's long black hair was plastered to her head by the rain. Durell weighed the Uzi in his hand.

"Come over!" he called.

"It's George!" Her face was stricken. "Please, help us!"

"Where is he?"

"At the house! Bring the car!"

Durell toed at a rock in the path, put down the Uzi, lifted the rock, and weighed it in both hands. Then he hurled it onto the bridge. For the instant that it sailed through the air, Lily Fan stared in horror. Then she turned and ran, and as the heavy rock landed on the bridge planking, she flung herself down on the wet grass beyond the opposite end of the span.

The explosion shook the earth.

The bridge lifted itself intact; then all at once it disintegrated into flying timbers and planks amid a great gush of smoke and flame. Durell threw himself sidewise, spotting moving shapes in the bamboo thickets across the gorge. He slammed the Uzi into automatic and squeezed the trigger; the rifle jumped and racketed, spraying the bamboo with slugs. He thought he heard someone scream over there, but then splinters and broken planks of the bridge rained down around him. He threw himself over Pala Mir to shelter her from the flying debris. The explosion rolled over them. He heard the sharp, heavy thud of one of the Rover's hunting rifles and turned his head. The Rajah still stood on his feet, tall and straight, his white hair wet in the rain. A man in khaki suddenly lurched up out of the bamboo across the gorge and tumbled down the bank. Another appeared and started to run away up the trail. Durell gave the Uzi another burst and saw more movement, a flash of white—and then there was silence.

The bridge was gone.

Pala Mir struggled under him, and he stood up.

"Are you all right?"

"Yes," she whispered. "Grandpapa?"

"I am just fine, child," said the old man. His rifle was in the crook of his elbow. "You saw it was a trap, Durell?"

"The bridge was rigged to blow up even under a single man's weight. I spotted the wire under the timbers."

Lily Fan still sprawled on the opposite edge of the ravine. She didn't move. Durell led the way down among the splintered remains of the bridge and climbed up toward the Chinese girl. She was still breathing. There was a gash on her forehead that bled freely, but it did not look serious. She moaned and rolled over, then looked up at him with wide eyes that reflected her fear.

"Please . . . I had to—"

"Who were those men?" he asked.

"Pao Thets. I'm not sure. They almost caught George at the plantation, and we became separated. They caught me and made me call to you to lure you onto the bridge."

"And where is George?"

"I don't know. He—he's like a demon. I never saw him like that before." Her mouth shook and she covered her face with her hands. "I'm sorry. They said they would—they would do awful things to me—and shoot me afterward if I didn't obey their orders. I'm sorry."

"Where is George heading?"

She looked at the Rajah. "To the mountain palace."

"Do you know why?"

"George didn't talk much. He is acting like a madman. He said he had to get there first, that is all."

"Did he set the drangh traps for me?"

"No! No, he wouldn't do that!"

"Was it the Pao Thets?"

"I—I suppose so."

She leaned shakily against him. He could feel every contour of her small, ripe body through her wet clothes. A warm, rain-filled wind blew the bamboo around them. There was no trace of the guerrillas except for two dead men, sprawled on the trail. The Rajah examined them clinically.

"These are not Malays," he said. "They come from much farther north. Their uniforms suggest a well-organized military supply. Their weapons are Chinese."

Durell nodded. Lily Fan had recovered, and the wound on her forehead was only a deep scratch.

He picked up his Uzi. "All right, let's see if we can catch up to George."

22

THE plantation house was empty and mournful in the persistent rain. From the knoll on which it stood, overgrown with vines and young saplings, the coastal lands below were lost in the blowing curtains of wetness. Durell scouted the place with care but found no traces of anyone except for the filth and debris left by the Pao Thets, who must have camped here. George Hammond was not in sight.

Satisfied, he returned to the porch where the trio huddled against the rain.

"Why is George in such a hurry to get to the hills?" he asked Lily Fan.

She was trying to braid her wet hair. "I told you, he was—how do you say—like a man possessed. He said—he said he had the answers and could prove he was right."

"Right about what?"

"Whatever he was working on, against you."

"We weren't working against each other."

"He felt that way, after—" She looked slyly at Pala Mir. "After he caught us in bed. He thought the worst of it, naturally, seeing us like that."

Pala Mir sniffed. Durell did not look at the other girl. "Lily, why did he take you along?"

"I knew the way better than he. But the guerrillas were always ahead of us. He was—he was so *angry*. He killed some of them on the river, and he—well, he was like a tiger in the jungle. I thought once he—he would kill even me."

"Why?"

"Well, I—I had a hard time keeping up with him."

Arranging packs, canteens, and cartridge bands, Pala Mir kept aloof from the talk. The Rajah helped her in dignified silence. The old man gained stature and dignity by the moment, as if his old royal prerogatives were reasserted. Not the smallest question in Durell's mind was Pala Mir. She had been remote since they started, even though the trip had begun on her initiative. Lily Fan was a sly little vixen but maybe merely adolescent. Just the same, he decided to watch her every moment.

For some miles beyond the rubber farm, the road was open and clear, and they made good time. As they climbed above the coastal plain, the air became cooler, although the rain went on. Durell felt caught between two demands—the need for care, lest they walk into another ambush, and the pressure of time, as the day waned and the clouds and rain darkened the sky.

Except for the trail, the country became the densest jungle Durell had ever seen. Vines blocked their way; insects were a constant torment; snakes, monkeys, and brilliant birds slithered, flashed, and chattered around them. By midafternoon they had to wade upstream in a small, greenish river, and leeches attacked them while the rain became a heavy pressure on their backs.

Although Pala Mir's face was strained, she showed no signs of weakening. Her stride steady, she worked silently beside Durell, hacking at the vines in their path. They had taken long parangs from the Rover to do the job, but it was backbreaking, slow work.

The afternoon waned.

Durell became concerned for the Rajah. The old man's face was grim, and he stumbled now and then and lagged behind. But he refused all offers of help when they started upward into the face of the monotonous rain.

"I'm perfectly fine," he gasped.

"You're not," Durell said. "I wish I could leave you somewhere, sir. This is too much for you."

"I will go anywhere you go, sir. This is my land, and I intend to do what is right for it, whatever the cost."

When the Rajah staggered and fell, Durell called a halt, and they ate the last of Pala Mir's sandwiches and drank more cold tea. Watching the trail, Durell sat with his back against a towering mahogany tree. Nothing stirred on the trail except a brightly colored snake that wriggled on about his business. Even the birds were silent.

He wondered how far ahead Hammond might be.

By four o'clock they were well into the foothills. The jungle was just as dense, the trail less defined, the rain endless. The Rajah was haggard, his face streaked with mud and scratches. Durell called another halt. The trail had followed a jungle ridge similar to the spine of a hog, but at this point the strangling growth gave way to a small clearing. He could see the countryside where it fell away to the eastern coast, lost in the blowing rain, and to the west and south, where the loom of the mountains bulked dark and grim. A series of valleys led upward into more jungle with a prominent gorge about five miles to the southwest, like a giant crack in the landscape.

Lily Fan came up silently and sat on her haunches, staring ahead. Her black hair was disheveled, but her round face was fresh. He turned and saw that Pala Mir was resting beside her grandfather and attending to his needs.

Lily moved her head in their direction. Contempt was acrid in her voice. "When the White Rajah was a young man, they say, he liked to come this way on elephants imported from Burma. And always with his pet tiger." She shivered suddenly. "Did you know there are still tigers sighted here? This is dreadful country."

"Have you been here before?" Durell questioned her.

"Only once with Paul in his plane. And once again with Paul in his car. I told George I wouldn't be much help." She wiped her forehead with the back of her hand. "Anyway, he didn't give me a choice. He *made* me come with him."

"Do you think he got away from the Pao Thets?"

She shivered. "Nothing could stop him. He—he wasn't human today. I never saw him like that."

"Did he talk much about me?" Durell asked.

"Just that he—he would stop you from getting to the mountain palace first."

"He thinks the palace has an answer for him?"

"I don't know what he's looking for or why. He'd never tell me that much, even though we were so—so intimate." Her almond eyes slid toward him. "I'm so afraid. The closer we get there, the more frightened I get." She sat closer to him. "I'm scared of you and George—of everything. I just don't understand what's going on." Her mouth trembling, she looked young and defenseless. "I'm sorry. I didn't know what I was getting into. It was fun with George; he's an American and very—very worldly, you know. I've never been anywhere outside of Pasangara. George said he would take me to the States one day. He kept promising me that, when—when he wanted me, and I wasn't sure—" She paused again and hung her head. "I'm just as bad as Pala Mir, I guess."

"Do you think Pala Mir is so bad?"

"Well, everybody knows how wild she was in Europe. But maybe I'm just as terrible a person as she is."

Pala Mir came over and regarded the lush, tiny Chinese girl with impersonal eyes. She spoke to Durell.

"My grandfather is having a difficult time, Sam. I hate to interrupt your tête-à-tête, but—"

"Can he go on?"

"I think so. It's about four miles more. You can see the palace through the binoculars when the rain lifts."

Durell scanned the opposite side of the valley near the gorge, as she indicated. The rain intervened. Then it lessened, and briefly he glimpsed a clearing and the bulk of a building on the cliff. Then it was gone. There were no villages in the valley and only a trace of the road that would be the main way in from the bus highway. Nothing moved that he could see, but that meant nothing; the jungle formed a canopy over most of the road.

"I don't see Paul's airstrip," he said.

"That's beyond the big gorge. There's a valley past it, quite lovely and surprising, about two miles from the palace itself." Pala Mir paused. "I don't see any signs of life over there at all."

Durell stood up and shouldered his pack and the Uzi. Lily Fan looked annoyed but stayed close to him.

Only two hours of daylight remained when they started up the opposite slope of the valley. High above, the remote palace of the White Rajah seemed to hang on the cliff amid mountain palms and dense bamboo. Long trailers of vines hung down the stone face of the mountain, and a stream made a silvery thread through the thick greenery.

They paused to rest, and the Rajah stood beside Durell. "It will be a difficult climb, but you are not to worry about me, sir. I will be all right, even if I fall behind. Pala Mir will help me. You and the little Chinese girl can go ahead if the trail is at all passable."

"Are those caves in the cliffs?" Durell asked, pointing to dark areas partly screened by the vines.

"Yes, some Buddhists used to live there, monks who came to meditate. They've been long deserted." The old man hesitated. "The palace itself was once a monastery, you see, before my father used it for a hunting lodge."

"Any connection between the caves and the palace?"

"There used to be. There were several tunnels to the caves, where the monks secluded themselves. The acolytes brought them food and water that way."

"Who knows about these tunnels?"

"No one, really."

"Has Pala Mir ever been in them?"

"Oh, no. I doubt if she ever heard of them."

The climb was not as difficult as it appeared. The

trail was clear and hard-packed, and the slackening rain did not interfere. Even so, a misty gloom filled the valley, and the Rajah's progress was even slower than he had promised. Presently he and Pala Mir were lost to sight beyond the twisting bends of the path. Durell found himself striding along with Lily Fan.

They were almost to the lowest cave when the girl stumbled, cried out, and almost slid from the path. Durell dropped the Uzi to grab for her, caught her hand, and hauled her back bodily. She sprawled breathlessly, then began to weep.

"Oh, my ankle—"

"Sit here." He placed her quickly against the wall of the cliff. Her skirt was torn and her face was scratched. Her eyes rolled wildly. "Don't faint," he snapped.

"I—I won't. I'm sorry."

"Can you stand up?"

"I don't think so."

"Try. You have to try."

She turned on him in tearful anger. "How can you be so brutal? I didn't *mean* to slip and fall, did I?"

"Did you?" he countered. "Now get on your feet."

Her mouth quivered. He looked back along the trail, but Pala Mir and the Rajah were not yet in sight. Above Durell and Lily was one of the dark openings in the cliff's face, one of the caves. The trail switched back about twenty yards from where they were and climbed steeply up to it.

"Come along. We'll rest up there."

"I—I'm afraid—"

"Of what?"

"I don't know—George, and you, and—"

He got her on her feet and she clung heavily to him. He kept one hand free for the Uzi, however, as they worked their way upward. He had to push the vines aside from the cave entrance. Lily Fan sat on the trail, shivering, looking down over the precipice to the valley below. Inside the cave there were old Buddhist relics, bones both human and animal, a grinning demon whose gilt face had long since eroded, and a series of erotic wall carvings. Trying not to breathe the foul air, Durell eased through the rubble. The cave came to a dead end. He was gone only three minutes when he returned to the trail.

Lily Fan had vanished.

Pala Mir and the Rajah were just catching up. They had not seen the Chinese girl. Durell swore and climbed up the path to the next cave entrance. Lily Fan was there, hands flat against the wall, her head turned to look for him.

She looked terrified. "George is in there. I can hear him. He—he'll think I deserted him. He'll kill me!"

"Why? He loves you, Lily."

"No. No, he doesn't." She was near tears again. Durell eased to the cave entrance and motioned her to be silent. She gulped and pushed her hair from her round face. "Please help me. I—I'm sorry about everything—"

"You knew what you were getting into when you started out with him," Durell said flatly.

"But I didn't! I had no idea he could be like this. So cold. Cruel. A maniac!" She spoke eagerly. "He tried to kill you when you were swimming in the canal after Pala Mir, did you know that? He shot at you with his rifle from the window after you left the apartment."

"All I know is that he missed."

He could hear nothing from inside the cave. He swung the Uzi to cover Lily and said, "You go in first."

"I couldn't!" she whispered desperately.

He pulled her to her feet and forced her toward the cave mouth. Pala Mir and the Rajah came up the trail and joined them again. The Rajah looked pale, plainly exhausted. There was a desperate, despondent look in his seamed face. Pala Mir looked at Durell and said, "What's happened?"

"Stay here with your grandfather. George Hammond is in the cave. Don't come in until I tell you."

"Are you taking Lily with you?"

"No, he's not!" Lily suddenly cried. Without warning she suddenly slipped out of Durell's grip and started to run up the path past the cave. Durell grabbed for her but missed. All hope of surprising Hammond was lost now in the noise he was forced to make. Maybe Lily Fan wanted it that way. He wasn't sure. He wasn't certain of anything at the moment. The Chinese girl was quick and elusive with no trace of injury that she had claimed. The trail took a sharp left turn and became a series of artificial steps cut into the rock. The girl scrambled up the series of low ledges with quick feet, not looking back.

"Lily!" he called.

He lifted the Uzi, then lowered it and halted. The base of the palace was only a hundred feet above, its stone foundations buttressed on top of the cliff. He could see no one up there, but he didn't dare raise his voice or fire a warning burst at the girl. He halted, frustrated. The girl vanished around another bend in the trail. He halted, watching the dusk gather in the valley. A bird cried somewhere, and a single pebble came bouncing down the cliff.

Pala Mir was hostile when he returned. "Is she gone?"

"She's gone."

"Sorry? She's just a little tart who made use of George Hammond to gratify her sense of importance."

"She's still Kuang's daughter. I feel a bit responsible for her."

"Yes, I could see that."

He wondered if Pala Mir was jealous or angry for other reasons. But he had no time to think about it. He turned to the cave, pondering whether or not Lily Fan had told the truth about Hammond being in there.

He didn't like to go in. Hammond had surely heard the noises they had made outside. He'd be waiting in there like a cunning, dangerous jungle animal. He wanted to avoid an ultimate meeting with the man who was acting like a renegade, but he couldn't avoid it.

He waved Pala Mir and the Rajah away from the cave, drew a deep breath, and stepped in.

23

MORE animal and human bones were strewn on the floor of this entry. Facing him in a niche cut into the rock was a long-forgotten shrine that encased the skeletons of a man and a woman engaged in exotic copulation. The stench inside made his stomach churn. There were ragged banners, a broken prayer wheel, a row of stone dragons, and a four-armed statue that indicated a mixture of Hindu and Buddhist beliefs.

Trying to fight his nausea, he flattened against the wall and listened. His fingers were damp on the Uzi trigger, so he shifted the gun to dry his fingers before he moved on. The dim light, made dimmer by the rain that still fell, only penetrated a few feet into the cavern.

At first he heard no sounds.

Then there was a sharp click that made him tense. The Uzi jerked upward. He was aware of an unusual tension in him. He'd never faced anyone quite like George Hammond before. Hammond knew every trick in the bag and had invented a few of his own, besides. If he'd gone over the edge in a rabid desire to prove himself, then he was even more dangerous than usual.

He heard another click.

Beyond the four-armed statue, the cave narrowed into a ragged crevice that led deeper into the cliff. It was only a vague, dark slot in the wall that grew darker by the moment as the daylight faded outside.

Click.

He thought of snakes, lizards, and jungle creatures

that might inhabit the hole; but the sound seemed to be metallic. Now he was sure Hammond was in there.

With a long stride he crossed the bone-strewn floor and flattened against the wall beside the crevice. It was some ten feet high but less than two feet wide. He would have to go in sidewise. If it were anyone but Hammond, he'd go in with the Uzi blazing. But he had to let George make the first strike.

He stepped into the crevice.

Nothing happened.

He waited, breathing lightly, aware of the dead air and the musty smell of long-rotted things on the stone floor. The darkness ahead was total. He felt the floor with his feet, took three steps inward, and halted. Water trickled somewhere. Suddenly, air fanned his cheek as he faced inward. He took another step, then went down on hands and knees in the rubble to feel the ground ahead an inch at a time as the narrow floor climbed steeply. He felt the trip wire brush his forearm as lightly as a fly.

The wire stretched from wall to wall about twelve inches from the floor. He stood up slowly with deliberate calculation. There were no other wires. Carefully, then, he stepped over it. A pebble grated slightly under his shoe.

He waited again. The cool draft of air against his face was stronger now.

Faint light glimmered above him.

He forced himself to breathe slowly. Sweat trickled down the nape of his neck. He wanted to call Hammond's name, but Hammond would know he was here. Hammond was waiting.

He moved up again, stepping sidewise in the narrow crevice. It felt like a coffin. He studied the walls in the faint light that now flickered down from above. It was not daylight. A heap of bones lay in his path, strewn for about three feet ahead. He put down the Uzi and considered them. They were human bones, very old, desiccated, and broken. A skull grinned up at him. He did not

want to step on the bones, and he could not see how
Hammond had crossed the debris without leaving some
trace of his passage.

Then he saw the long femur bone, angled upward,
just where he would have put his foot for the next step.
One end was lodged in the wall, and he saw how it could
act as a lever with his weight on the other end. A small
chimney of bolders and rocks would be dislodged, perhaps bringing the whole tunnel down on his head.

Durell picked up the Uzi again and stepped around
and over the booby trap.

The light was brighter. It flickered with a pale yellow
wash over the rocky walls. There were dark niches to
the right, and some contained grotesque statues with
monstrous leers and frowns, demons calculated to frighten
any who dared to intrude this far. The slope of the floor
lifted sharply, and Durell found himself staring into a
larger cavern. No one was in it. A candle guttered on the
floor, and there was a haversack, canvas-covered boxes,
and a rifle piled beside the candle. The cave tunnel went
on from the other side into the darkness again.

He turned carefully to face the way he had come. He
had a hard time controlling a sudden surge of panic.

"Come on out, George," he said quietly.

He saw the glint of Hammond's gun first. Hammond
stepped out of one of the niches he had just passed. He
felt no chagrin that George had gotten behind him. Durell
looked at the gaunt man, looked at his gun, then at his
eyes.

They looked insane. Durell put down his Uzi.

"Smart fellow," Hammond said.

"How many did you kill to get this far?"

"Six. Seven. I didn't think you'd make it, Cajun."

Durell moved his head. "What's upstairs?"

"Pao Thets. They use the palace as an HQ."

"You've been up there?"

"Sure. It's an arms depot, a field hospital, barracks.
You name it. A regular commando base for murder."

"Where did they come from?"

Hammond shrugged. "Hanoi sent them. Or maybe Peking. It's all the same, isn't it? Step back a bit, Cajun, over there against the wall."

Durell did as he was told.

"Where are the others?" Hammond asked.

"Outside the cave. We ran into Lily Fan."

Hammond's deep-sunk eyes glittered. "The bitch. I should've killed the little bitch."

"She crossed you?"

"Yes, she crossed me. You're lucky. You got rid of her and you're still alive."

Durell said, "I thought you were crazy about her."

"I'm not crazy about anybody in this world." Hammond looked mad enough to destroy everything in his rage. His madness made him more dangerous because all his cunning, technique, and professionalism in this business had come to the fore. Durell said, "Can I put down my hands?"

"Don't touch your knife. I can see it there in the right-hand pocket. Have you any TH-3's?"

"Thermits? Yes. I've no quarrel with you, George."

"Well, I do with you. I ought to wipe you, right now. I don't need any help, but—"

"But—?"

Hammond grinned. "The noise, buddy-wuddy. There are two hundred Pao Thets just over our heads. Of course, I could do it quietly with my hands—"

"Don't try it. I don't want to kill you."

"You couldn't."

"I could, George."

The older man breathed a bit too quickly, his thin face strained and became taut, his limp more pronounced as he moved around the small heap of equipment he had left on the cave floor. There was a slight quiver in Hammond's hand as he rammed his gun into Durell's belly.

Durell said, "You're too close to me, George. You know that's not proper procedure. They don't teach us that any more. Stand your distance."

"You're a pretty smart cookie, Cajun."

"What happened to Chiang Gi? Who killed him?"

"Who do you think?" Hammond countered.

"It wasn't you."

"Hell, no. He was useful."

"It was Paul Merrydale," Durell said.

"That's right."

"It's been young Merrydale all along?"

"That should be no surprise," Hammond said.

"And Tileong?"

"He'll be here. I think he's around somewhere, right now."

"With Paul?"

"He's walking into a trap. He doesn't know how strong the guerrillas are. He thinks it'll be a piece of cake."

"And the Thrashers?"

"Haven't seen them or the pilots." Hammond sounded angry. "I've wasted a lot of time trying to keep you off my tail, Cajun. This is my game, understand? I've waited a long time for this chance. All those long-haired psychiatrists saying I was knocked off-balance, claiming I'm too trigger-happy, too hungry to kill, too *old* to stay in the business! I'll show the lot of them, the bastards. I'll let them hear my name again, you can bet on it."

"Take it easy, George."

"Don't patronize me!" Hammond shouted. He stepped back. The gun in his hand trembled violently for a moment. His craggy face looked like death's head in the guttering light of the candle on the floor. Then suddenly he grinned, reached in his khaki shirt, and took out one of his thin Dutch cigars. His eyes never left Durell's face as he snapped a wooden match aflame on his thumb nail.

"You knew I was waiting for you near the Land Rover last night?" he asked, his voice suddenly quiet.

"I smelled your cigar smoke," Durell said.

"And you thought I was trying to knock you over when you played Sir Galahad and dived into the canal for Pala Mir?"

"Your aim was just a bit off."

"There's nothing wrong with my aim. Nothing at all. You were dead in my sights. Dead, buddy-wuddy. But I figured you might be useful, somehow. I changed my mind several times since then, trying to stop you from getting here."

"We still have to work together, George."

"Why?" Hammond asked flatly. "It's my game."

"I'm thinking of the pilots."

"Who?"

"The Thrasher pilots. I think they're still alive. Maybe they're prisoners upstairs in the palace."

"No, they're not there. They're dead, chum."

"Are you sure?"

"It's an educated guess. Why should the Pao Thets keep 'em and feed 'em?"

Durell was stubborn. "I think they're alive, and it's our job to get them out of here."

"And?"

"And get the Judas pilot who used the stolen Navy Boomerang devices to throw the Thrasher navigation instruments out of whack so they had to follow the Judas instead of getting back to the carrier."

"You figured that all out?"

"It was obvious," Durell said.

"And who is the Judas?"

"Sometimes it's Paul," Durell said. "But not the last time, because he was with Pala Mir at her river house when I first met her."

Hammond grinned. "That's right."

"Do you know the other one, then?"

Hammond lowered his gun and backed away, the cigar clenched in his yellowish teeth. His eyes were hidden in the shadows of their deep sockets under his bushy brows. He limped to the canvas-covered equipment he had put on the cave floor, hefted his gun, and looked sharply at Durell.

"I ought to wipe you, really, here and now."

"You can't," Durell said.

"Why not?"

"The Rajah is behind you with his rifle. He's still a crack shot. He got through your booby traps, too."

Hammond stood very still. Something like despair glittered in his eyes, but then he said, "I don't care if it is a bluff. I'm tired." He put down his gun, turned his back on Durell and the crevice, and began unpacking the small cases he had brought with him.

Durell let out his breath. It seemed as if he had been holding it for an eternity.

"My Uzi?" he said.

"Them Israelis make a nice machine," Hammond said. "Pick it up. And take some of these grenades. Tell that old coot to put down his elephant gun. I've got to find Lily Fan."

24

THEY drank lukewarm tea out of battered tin cups, the water heated by one of Durell's Thermit sticks. Pala Mir sat cross-legged on the floor, her lovely face impassive in the candlelight. The Rajah stood at the far end of the cave where a flight of rough steps carved out of the rock led up to the lower levels of his former palace.

Durell wished he could read Hammond's face. The hatred and envy were still there. He had the feeling that Hammond was strung out at the end of a long, taut wire and that the wire would soon snap.

"I've been listening to the gooks up there," Hammond said, jerking his thumb upward. His speech was tight and precise, but he did not look at Durell. He kept watching Pala Mir's quiet face. "We have to get through the gorge to the airfield. It's guarded, of course, and there's a village at one end that we'll have to pass. The Malays there are practically prisoners, used for labor services by the Pao Thets. I've already been through the gorge and back. I came back to wait for you, Cajun." He grinned but with a senseless grimace that was not sane. "The old man won't be able to make it."

The Rajah said quietly, "I came this far, sir, and do not intend to stop. This is my province whether I once ruled it or whether I am just another citizen. But I would like to ask a question."

Hammond shrugged. "Go ahead."

"You said Tileong will be here with his troops. They are well trained for guerrilla warfare. Why do we not wait for his reinforcements?"

"We can't wait," Hammond said. "They're taking the Thrasher jets to bomb Pasangara at dawn, as a start of their campaign to turn Pasangara into a so-called People's Democratic Republic. Semantics, of course. It will be ruled by Peking via Hanoi. The Peking emperors, just like the new Soviet czars, are always hungry for new lands to ruin."

"But if they use U. S. Navy planes—" the Rajah paused, and his face went gray.

"Exactly. The world would never get the facts straight afterward. But your grandson, Paul, hopes to be named— ah—premier. It's his dream to regain power for the Merrydale name—even if he is an emperor's puppet."

The Rajah picked up his rifle with a trembling hand, then put it down again. Pala Mir moved closer to him. The old man started to speak, looked helpless, and then lowered his head.

"I'm very sorry to hear this about Paul."

"So you'd better stay behind," Hammond said bluntly.

"No, Mr. Hammond. One must do what one's conscience dictates. If Paul is at the heart of this, then he is one of the enemy."

"I intend to kill him," Hammond said. He looked utterly cruel. "Do you still want to come along?"

The Rajah nodded.

They moved in single file up the narrow steps of the lower levels of the mountain palace. There were long, dank corridors, all empty; a few doors that the Rajah indicated could be opened; and empty, cavernous storage rooms. From up above, once, they heard a burst of drunken laughter, and one time they heard a single shot.

Hammond led the way. Durell was the rear guard. Windows opened out on the valley, showing the mist of deep dusk. There was less than half an hour of daylight left.

At the top of a final stairway, a door led them to a weed-grown garden. There was a smell of camp smoke and wet vegetation in the air. It had stopped raining, and the heavy trees dripped somberly on the once-elegant paths.

Hammond held up a warning hand. They halted. The sound of men talking came clearly to them. Just beyond the door to the garden was a small bamboo chair.

Lily Fan sat there. She looked dejected.

A small, bandy-legged guerrilla stood nearby, smoking and talking to her.

Hammond's breath made a thin sound. "We have to get out this way. And I want that girl."

"We can go around somehow," Durell said.

"No. I want her. The bitch. She's been Paul's mistress all along. Pumping me for all she could learn out of the consulate's security files. Handing it over to the Pao Thets via Paul."

"Let it go," Durell said.

Hammond shivered, staring at the sloe-eyed Chinese girl. Durell pushed Hammond's gun down. "Not that way, George."

"You're right," Hammond agreed quietly.

Before Durell could check him again, Hammond stepped calmly out into the garden. The guard turned, his flat face wrinkled with astonishment. Before the man had any chance to shout or raise his gun, Hammond was around and behind him, the barrel of his rifle pulled hard across the other's throat, while Hammond jammed his knee into the man's kidneys. Lily Fan started to rise, terror in her eyes, but Durell jumped and caught her arm as she swung about, clapped a hand over her mouth, and checked her scream. There was a crunching sound as the guerrilla's throat was crushed. Lily wriggled like an eel in Durell's grip. Hammond let the dead man slide to the ground and swung to face the girl. His face was dark with rage. Durell lifted Lily Fan bodily aside, still muffling her mouth.

"Don't kill her, George."

Hammond shook like a tree in a high wind. His gaunt face looked ashen; his blood-dark eyes regarded the terrified girl for a moment, and then the Rajah stepped forward.

"I believe," he said gently, "we had all best leave this place before we are seen."

The trail through the gorge was difficult. Evening mists clung to the rocky scarps, permeating the vines that fell hundreds of feet downward. A small stream thundered far below. It began to rain again.

Lily Fan was forced to go first with her hands tied behind her and a gag in her mouth. Small whimpering sounds came from her throat. Directly behind her, Hammond forced them on at a cruel pace, his limp more exaggerated but his steps sure and quick.

The rain pounded their backs, the darkness grew more ominous, and then it ended. A long streak of golden sunlight shot through the rolling mountain clouds. They had come to the end of the gorge.

The path widened, and they stood several hundred feet above the main road that entered the valley. Bamboo and vines screened them from a small hut down the slope where two or three small men with slung rifles stood looking at the rainbow that now arched across the sky.

Mist lifted like steam from the sodden earth. It was a reprieve, Durell thought; they still had enough daylight left.

"Hold it here," he said.

Hammond, who had started down, pushing Lily ahead, turned an angry hatchet face toward him. "What for?"

"Take it easy, George."

"Listen, I know the way—"

"But we don't."

Hammond shrugged, staring out over the valley. Durell took the Rajah's binoculars and considered the problem spread out below them. The airstrip was at the far end of the mile-long valley floor, and it had been developed into the equivalent of an aircraft-carrier deck slashed out of the surrounding jungle. At the near end of the valley the road went through a small village on the banks of a mountain stream. Durell scanned the single street and saw several moving figures, but he could not determine if they were Pao Thet or civilian. Parked at one end of the airstrip was a twin-engined Beechcraft— Paul Merrydale's—and close by was a thatched hangar for it.

At first, he could not determine the other buildings hidden under their camouflage of vines. Then he suddenly discerned the spider-web tower of a radio transmitter above the foliage. Lowering the glasses, he saw the shapes of long native-type barracks leap into recognition. Several men lounged there, eating, with their weapons beside them. Under the camouflage net the earth was pounded flat, as if the guerrilla base had been established here for some time. He swung the glasses back to the end of the airstrip to study the jungle again, found the wide trail, and even made out the drag traces where aircraft had been hauled off the strip out of sight. He could not see any Thrashers; but he knew they were there.

The thick jungle all around the valley looked safe enough. He wondered if Tileong and his antiterrorist people had arrived, and if so, where they might be.

"Come on, let's move," Hammond said harshly. He knelt on the trail and opened his pack, displaying half a dozen grenades and Thermit bombs, which he stuffed into the big pockets of his bush jacket. Nervous energy vibrated all around his tall, gray figure. He seemed transformed by the prospect of violent action ahead. Durell checked him and said, "I'll take half the grenades."

"What for? I can handle this alone."

"But you're not alone. It's a job for both of us, remember?"

Hammond's eyes were bleak. "All right. We'll eliminate the village first—"

"No. The pilots have first priority," Durell said. "Some of them have been prisoners here for weeks."

"Then they're dead."

"Maybe not. But if we blow the village first, we still have half a mile to get to the barracks at the other end of the field. Enough time for the Pao Thets to put bullets into their necks."

Hammond straightened, scanning the valley before him. The clouds were shredding, and the sun was pouring in from the west. Mists moved over the jungle down there. "I told you," Hammond said, "I've already scouted the place. I'll lead the way. Just do as I say."

"We'll go together," Durell said.

"I'm going to scrub that son of a bitch Paul," Hammond said. "With extreme prejudice, as the office says."

Durell looked for Pala Mir and the Rajah. Hammond had not tried to lower his voice. Lily Fan was watching him, her eyes filled with horror that certainly was not faked now. Over the gag stuffed in her mouth, she seemed to be straining to speak to him. He stared into her black eyes, and she blinked them rapidly, as if fighting back tears. But then Pala Mir spoke quietly.

"Mr. Hammond, whatever my brother's faults and mistakes, Paul is not an animal to be hunted down."

Hammond spoke ferociously. "Your brother is a vermin, a traitor to Pasangara. He betrayed you and your grandfather and put the whole province in jeopardy. I'm going to kill him."

"He should be allowed a trial," the girl said evenly. "It's you who's acting like a mad dog."

Hammond grinned meaninglessly but made no reply. Durell took four of the grenades and pocketed them. The Rajah coughed. He looked better, despite their grueling race through the gorge.

"If I might make a suggestion—"

"No, sir," Hammond said bluntly. "This is my game. I'm in command. Durell has been assigned to me, and all of you will do as I say. I won't allow any foul-ups. I'd rather you all stayed right here until I'm finished down there. I can do it better alone. If you think—"

"I know a way around the village," said the old man. "I merely wish to end this tragedy as quickly as we can."

Hammond weighed his automatic, then said, "We'll see. As far as I'm concerned, you're all just excess baggage. But I can't leave you here. One false break, though, and you get it. I don't tolerate any slip-ups."

Pala Mir looked at Durell, as if expecting him to challenge Hammond. But Durell's face was like stone.

They started down into the valley.

The descent was easy enough under the canopy of dripping trees. It was half a mile down to the trail that entered the village. Again, Hammond went first, almost dragging Lily Fan with him. Durell acted as rear guard, and presently Pala Mir joined him. She moved lithely, apparently not fatigued by the long day. She had bound up her dark hair in a roll of cloth, and without makeup her beauty had a calm simplicity. Her dark blue eyes, however, reflected small clouds of worry that came and went.

"Is he serious?" she asked. "About killing Paul?"

"He's done such things before," Durell murmured.

"But then—he's just a brutal murderer."

"We all are," said Durell.

She did not look at him. "Have you had assignments— where you were an assassin?"

"I've killed men," he said simply.

"When it was not necessary?"

"No. Only when needed."

"But Hammond is—"

"I know."

"Will you help me, Sam? I can't let it happen!"

"Wait," he said.

She walked on beside him for a bit, then said, "Something is not right, you know."

"That's true."

"It's as if the perspective of things is somehow distorted. I can't explain it. It's just a feeling I have."

"I have the same feeling," he said.

25

THROUGH a tall screen of green bamboo, glistening with diamond-like drops in the lowering rays of the setting sun, they studied the road two hundred yards from the village. A woman in a sarong with breasts bared to an infant hurried across the dirt street and vanished into one of the huts. Her brown face was sullen. A battered Coca Cola sign, an American gift to Malay culture, hung askew over a tiny shop. No men were in sight. The river ran fast and white after the recent rain, making white teeth that gnawed at the poles along its banks.

Closer at hand, a mortar crew of three guerrillas with Chinese weapons squatted in the road while cooking rice over a small fire. Wearing black pajamas, they looked small but alert.

Hammond waved a hand downward, and they moved left along the road until the crew was out of sight. When they came upon a solitary guard who was sitting with his back against a flame tree and sucking at a cigarette, Hammond signaled to Durell. Durell stepped onto the road and said quietly, "Hey."

The man looked up, his slanted eyes widening with shock. Then Hammond came up behind him, and there was a small thudding sound as the knife went in. The man's legs buckled and he went down in silence.

"All right," Hammond whispered. "Everybody across."

Lily Fan stumbled and sprawled in the mud as Hammond shoved her. Durell helped her up. The others crossed swiftly and silently, and once more the bamboo swallowed them. In another moment they were at the river.

The Rajah crossed the swift current first, rifle held high over his white head. Pala Mir followed; then Hammond slung Lily Fan over one shoulder and forged through the rushing water. Durell came last. As he climbed up the steep bank, he stared into Hammond's grin, then at his gun.

"Company ahead, buddy-wuddy."

"How many?"

"Plenty."

"Any ideas?"

"We'll get through. Make it fast."

"Point that gun somewhere else, George."

"Are you nervous, Cajun?"

"I'm always nervous."

There was an aura of tension, even joy, about Hammond in the prospect of action. His teeth were bared behind skinned-back lips. He swung ahead, limping, with a grenade in his hand. Durell caught up with him in two long strides.

"Hold it now, George, right here. I told you, I want those pilots safe."

"So?"

"So, no noise. No grenades yet."

At that moment came a different voice. "Excellent thought, Mr. Durell."

Colonel Tileong stepped from the jungle brush.

Pasangára's security chief looked as cool and tidy, as if he were seated behind his office desk. Instead of a business suit, however, he wore jungle fatigues, boots, and a beret with an impressive medallion on it. He carried an American M-16 rifle. Out of the jungle around him, as soundlessly as ghosts, rose a squad of his men, similarly armed. They looked efficient. Lieutenant Parepa slid effortlessly into sight, his bulk quiet, his face sweaty.

"Hey, American," he called to Durell. He pointed his rifle at him. "I kill you any time, last ten minute, you like that? We watch you come all way down, buddy-wuddy, *tuan.*"

"Still a joker, Parepa," Durell said. "You'll get your teeth knocked in, waving that gun around."

"You nervous, hey?"

Durell sighed.

Colonel Tileong touched his moustache, looked at an ornate wristwatch, and said crisply, "We have over an hour of operational daylight left. I have been expecting you for this past hour, Mr. Durell." He smiled briefly. "Your consul, Mr. Condon, briefed me on your mission here. I might say that we are allies on this venture."

"Good," Durell said flatly.

"My men are highly trained and ready. We mean to wipe out the Pao Thets without mercy, something I have been organizing for some time. I must thank you and your colleague, Mr. Hammond, for leading the way and providing some answers."

Hammond grunted impatiently. "Look, Tileong, we have our own job to do. We don't want interference."

"I am sorry, but that is precisely what you shall get," Tileong said quietly. "The operation will follow my plan." He looked sharply at Lily Fan. "What is the trouble with the young lady?"

"She works with Paul Merrydale and the Pao Thets,"

Hammond snapped. "I'd have shot her but the Cajun has a soft heart."

Lily Fan looked terrified again.

"And," Hammond added, "she is my prisoner."

Tileong said gently, "I regret, sir, you forget you are in Pasangara. You also forget that she is the daughter of our premier, Mr. Kuang. He is the supreme authority here. You will turn the young lady over to me, and we will listen to her side of it in good time."

"Look here, Tileong—" Hammond began.

Durell intervened. "Colonel, my sole aim is to get to the American Navy pilots who are prisoners at the other end of the airfield in those barracks. Your aim is to clean out the Pao Thets. We can divide our goals that way."

Parepa snorted. He looked eager and bloodthirsty. Tileong waved a few of his men forward into the jungle, and the men moved out efficiently. They had been well trained.

Tileong said, "I know little about the pilots. If you and Hammond wish to go ahead, you may. Lieutenant Parepa will accompany you, but I cannot spare any men for the first part of the operation. There are over two hundred Pao Thets here, and I have only fifty in my company. Still," he added, smiling grimly, "I believe the odds are in my favor."

Hammond nodded. "Fine. Let's get going. And Lily?"

"The girl remains with me," Tileong said. He indicated his armed men. "Will you argue about it, sir?"

Hammond grinned his insane grin. "Okay, but she's a rebel bitch, Tileong, and you ought to shoot her right now."

"She is the premier's daughter."

Pala Mir spoke up. "May I go with you, Sam?"

"Stay with your grandfather," he said shortly.

Parepa said, "Hurry up, buddy-wuddy, *tuan*."

The three men moved quickly along the opposite slope of the valley above the airstrip. The village was not as empty as it had appeared. There were a number of Pao

Thets quartered there, and the Malays, finished with their day's labor, were being herded into a fenced compound. Hammond walked with a long tiger's stride, like a stalking jungle animal. Durell matched him in silence and speed. Parepa was a little clumsy and once stumbled on a vine, setting off a series of crackling noises. Hammond turned a furious face toward him.

"Hell, you'd better stay away from me. You and Durell take off that way. When you hear my first shot, get into the barracks first."

Durell kept silent and did not object, for reasons of his own. Parepa grinned, taunting him. "You take orders from Hammond, *tuan?* I think maybe you like sore bellies and beating up, hey?"

Durell said nothing but he and Parepa continued to follow Hammond.

There were two vehicles parked under camouflage at the end of the airstrip—a towing jeep and a command car. Guards stood about, smoking and talking quietly in the evening dusk. A squad of guerrillas marched across the field and vanished into the opposite jungle. The dim sound of metal striking metal came through the foliage.

Lying flat on his belly, Hammond wriggled forward along a rise and parted the grass for a better view.

"I guess the planes, the Thrashers, are hauled off under the nets across the way. Do you see the tracks where the jets were dragged off the runway?"

"I see them," Durell said.

"We can forget about the planes. If it's true the Pao Thets are going to bomb Pasangara tonight, they'll wait another hour, at least." Hammond looked at his watch and squinted at the loom of the mountain to the west. The sun had gone behind it, and the sky was streaked with orange and lilac colors. "Fifteen minutes. I figure five to reach the prison compound. It will be just ahead where the jeeps are parked. We'll come around from the other side. You and Parepa move in from this direction. At 8:10 we bust the place open."

They hurried along a narrow trail above the airstrip. After two minutes they came to a barbed-wire fence, seven feet tall. Hammond waved Durell one way and went the other, vanishing within a few steps. Durell checked the wire, saw no electronic telltales. He heard a soft *spang!* and Hammond appeared briefly, waving a wire cutter. They were through the fence a moment later.

The smell of burning charcoal hung in the quiet evening air. Laughter could be faintly heard. A hundred more yards brought them to the edge of a clearing just beyond the end of the airstrip. They had to go on their bellies now. A second fence barred their way.

Below them and to the right was a prison compound.

Parepa hissed with satisfaction. No doubt, Durell thought, he admired the efficiency of the Pao Thet prison.

There were triple fences of barbed wire about a small rectangle of trampled earth and mud that contained a tiny row of huts not much larger than doghouses. A single bigger building, obviously serving as a mess hall, stood against one side of the inner fence.

Only one watchtower, mounting a thatched-roof platform, patrolled by a guard with a .50 machine gun, was situated at the south end of the compound rectangle.

Disconsolate and despondent, the men, wearing tattered black pajamas and headcloths, were squatting in the mud or simply standing idly, staring into the green jungle.

"How many do you make?" Hammond whispered.

"Ten outside," Durell said.

"Two more in the cook hut, I think. I'll circle around and come in that way, through the wire and over the roof of the hut. You and Parepa take the main gate."

Durell nodded and watched Hammond lift himself up and wriggle through the barbed wire; he disappeared in a flash into the brush beyond. Parepa grunted again and reached in a Claymore pouch for a grenade.

"We go now, hey?"

"Give him time," Durell said.

"He great fighter. Like goes amok, hey?"

"Like, yes," Durell said.

When his sweep-second hand showed the right time, Durell moved to the right along the wire fence, tending downward toward the beaten trail that led to the main gate under the watchtower. Now and then through the foliage he glimpsed the prisoners, who rarely moved about. He breathed easier when the missing two appeared from the cook hut and joined the others in the compound.

"Over there," Parepa whispered.

Durell halted. Parepa moved silently through the jungle, his huge hands holding his M-16, now set on automatic. His mouth grinned, but his eyes were bleak, regarding Durell.

"We get better field of fire on sentry in tower," Parepa said. Then he added softly, "Hey, you still sore at me, American?"

"What for?"

"Me beating you. Was Tileong's orders."

"I know."

"Well, you still sore?"

"No."

"That's good. I no like man to die angry with me. You die now, hey? Surprise?"

"No."

"I have gun at your head."

"And I have a grenade."

Durell produced the grenade which he had been holding in his left hand. He pulled the pin and held it out on his palm toward Lieutenant Parepa.

Parepa's dark brown eyes grew wide with shock, disbelief, astonishment, then abject fear. The M-16 in his big paws wavered. His mouth opened, closed, opened again.

"You blow us both up?" Parepa whispered.

"That's right, buddy-wuddy."

"No!" Parepa shouted. "No! Crazy!"

The big Malay stumbled and turned, running headlong through the jungle, down toward the compound. He screamed once, as if calling Hammond, and then Durell lobbed the grenade after him.

It went off with a dull roar that shattered the stillness of the little valley.

At the same time, there was another series of concussions from the village—the sudden rattle of automatic fire, the thump of grenades, the whomp of a mortar. Durell stood still, his head turned, watching smoke mushroom over the settlement. It would be Tileong, he thought. He didn't want to move. He was covered with sweat, and his hand shook slightly as he lifted the Uzi again. It had been a close call. He seemed to see nothing but the bore of Parepa's M-16, pointed right between his eyes, and the flash of Parepa's big white teeth behind it, smiling at his death.

He told himself again to move, and for a moment he couldn't. But then he turned and ran in the same direction Parepa had gone, toward the stockade.

26

PAREPA was dead, sprawled in a tangle of limbs from the grenade thrown at him. Durell ran past him, crouching, holding the Uzi close to avoid tangling with the vines, sliding this way and that through the thick growth. There was shouting from the stockade, then a single shot. From the right near the airstrip came the thump of an exploding mortar shell. It was almost dark under the canopy of the jungle trees, but daylight filtered through from the clearing ahead. Durell slid under another barbed-wire fence. Flat on his stomach, moving fast, he came up behind a wild oleander, choked with tiny orchids about to open for the evening. Something slid away along the jungle floor, a flicker of brown and red. He did not know what it was.

There was fighting going on in the village behind him where Tileong's men had either been surprised or gone on to attack, regardless of the schedule. Durell saw the guard on the stockade tower lean over the rail; he yelled to someone behind the fence. Durell looked for the pilots, and seeing them being herded toward one side of the compound, he swore softly. Five Pao Thets held guns on the captive Americans. The guard in the tower swiveled his machine gun to cover them, too.

He cocked the Uzi on automatic and waited. There was no sign of Hammond, coming in over the cook-hut roof as he had promised.

"Sam?"

It was the faintest of whispers, but his weapon came up instantly, covering the jungle at his back.

"It's me. Pala Mir. And Grandpapa."

"Come out here," he whispered harshly.

"Don't shoot, please. Trust me."

"Show yourself."

The girl and the Rajah stepped carefully into view. The Rajah still carried his hunting rifle. The girl had armed herself with an M-16, and he wondered briefly where she had gotten it. She had a sack of Claymore bombs slung over her shoulder. Her face was scratched and her long hair had become tangled. Peering at the stockade, she knelt beside him.

"Where is Parepa?"

"Dead. He tried to kill me."

"He—but why?"

Durell waved toward the stockade. "We're almost too late. Tileong blew the whistle on us. Too eager to get his Pao Thets cleaned out, I guess."

"And Hammond?"

"No show, as yet."

From the screen of brush, the ground sloped down across a clearing thick with waist-high saw grass, banking a tiny stream that flowed near the compound gate. There was no cover for them over the fifty yards leading to the watchtower. The guard up there under his thatched roof

was watching the prisoners being herded against the opposite wire fence. He kept fanning his machine gun, as if
impatient to squeeze the trigger and open fire.

"What are they doing?" Pala Mir whispered.

"Getting ready for a massacre."

There was more fighting, sounds of explosions, and
rapid-fire automatics in the village beyond the airstrip
half a mile away. It was growing heavier. Grenades
slammed and mortars whomped, and the evening breeze
brought the smell of smoke and fire through the foliage.

Durell watched the thatched roof of the cook shed on
the opposite side of the compound. It was 8:11. Hammond was late.

The Rajah coughed. "May I go on with you, Durell?"

Durell looked at him. The old man had recovered from
their long trek, and although his face was still seamed by
exhaustion, there was pride and determination in him.

"We have to wait," Durell said.

"But those guards will kill your Navy pilots—"

"I think not."

The prisoners were lined up against the wire fence.
Even from here, Durell could see in their attitudes that
they expected death. The guards were shouting and harry-
ing them into place, and an officer in a khaki uniform
turned his head to yell something to the machine gunner
in the watchtower. The guard grinned, swinging his weapon back and forth.

Durell lifted the Uzi and squeezed the trigger.

The sudden roar of the automatic froze everyone in the
compound. He kept firing at the tower. He heard the
Rajah's heavy rifle thump once, but he didn't know if it
was his Uzi or the Rajah's shot that got the man, who
threw up his arms, spun around, broke through the flimsy
rail of his platform, and fell to the ground.

Durell got up and ran through the tall grass for the
gate. Pala Mir ran beside him. The Rajah moved slower,
covering their rear. At the same time, Hammond finally
appeared on the roof of the shed on the other side of the
clearing.

Durell threw his first grenade and blew the gate apart. He heard a yell from the top of the shed and saw Hammond, his legs spread wide, holding his rifle at hip height and spraying the running guards. The captive pilots had thrown themselves flat in a line along the fence.

Durell rushed through the gate, the Uzi chattering, then turned left along the fence. A Pao Thet charged at him with a bayonet. He ducked left, brought the Uzi up with a sharp sweep that knocked aside the blade, then reversed the gun, smashing it at the guerrilla's shaven skull. The man went down and Pala Mir jumped over him to join Durell. The Rajah's heavy hunting rifle boomed again, and a Pao Thet who was taking aim at Hammond's figure atop the shed suddenly spun about, as if kicked by a mule, and rolled over and over, his weapon firing into the mud.

The guerrillas, caught in a cross fire between Hammond and Durell, scattered, running this way and that. Seeking escape, they finally came at the gate. Hammond's gun slammed again, and Durell threw another grenade. He heard Pala Mir firing, too, and then he ran farther along the fence.

A scarecrow figure rose up from the mud ahead, face darkened by dirt but teeth showing in a grin.

"Hey, chum! Glad to see you!"

The remains of a JG's bar on a khaki shoulder hung loose by a thread. The captive yelled to his fellow prisoners, and Durell gave him a grenade. "Pick up any weapons you can find."

"We getting out, sir?"

"Yes. But you'll have to help."

"It's a pleasure."

The shed on which Hammond had been standing suddenly went up with a tremendous explosion. But Hammond was already gone from there. The gush of flame and smoke gave the Pao Thets a chance to pour through the compound gate. Durell let them go, helping the prisoners arm themselves. In just the brief days and weeks they had been kept here, they already looked like ragged ghosts.

But now their haunted eyes were suddenly aflame with hope they had thought was lost forever.

The JG said, "The Thrashers are over there, sir. The gooks lured us—God knows how—to this hell hole. We don't even know where we are."

"You're on your way home," Durell said.

One of the pilots had a broken leg; another showed scars from torture. Several of them trembled from weakness, derived from beatings and starvation. But they snatched up the weapons dropped by the fleeing Pao Thets and followed Durell, Pala Mir, and the Rajah as quickly as they could.

Durell searched for Hammond.

The Pao Thets had disappeared. The shed was in flames. Through the smoke Durell could see Hammond's lean figure leap from a fence rail, his gun held high. Swinging toward the end of the airstrip, Hammond raised his hand, then turned away from Durell and the freed captives. There were more sheds here, and machine-gun fire was coming from them. Hammond went flat on his belly, out of sight in the tall grass. A grenade sailed through the air, his arm briefly visible, and a gout of flame came from the nearest shed. One of the machine guns went silent.

"Hammond!" Durell shouted. "Get back!"

He knew that Hammond heard him, but the man made no effort to return. He went under the fence on the airfield side, charging the enemy positions alone.

The Navy pilots started forward. The young JG said, "I don't know who you are, sir, but—thanks. What can we do to help?"

"Come along," Durell told them. "Those of you who are fit enough and have some guns."

"We'll manage. We owe these people something."

Durell went off ahead with Pala Mir keeping pace with him. He looked at her smudged face and said angrily, "This is no place for you. Get back there."

"I want to find Paul!"

"So do I. Especially before Hammond gets to him."

"But I don't think George will—"

"He will," Durell said flatly.

Her face went white under the smudges. The sky was almost dark now, and the red glare of the burning prison shed cast an unearthly glow on the compound and shadowed jungle. Durell quickly crossed the prison yard, skirted the burning shed, and found the broken wire where Hammond had gone. The airfield was a short distance beyond. To the left farther in the jungle were long native sheds with glints and glimmers of giant metal shapes.

"The Thrashers," he said.

"Would they really use them to bomb Pasangara?"

"One or two, anyway. Paul is a qualified pilot."

"But Paul wouldn't—"

"Not now, he won't."

He saw the private Beechcraft pulled off the strip into the brush at the other side of the field. There was fighting going on at the other end of the valley. Probably Tileong's men, he thought. He searched for Hammond but couldn't see him in the dusk.

"George!" he called again.

There was a sudden burst of fire from the right. He pulled Pala Mir down with him, and the slugs ripped and slashed through the foliage overhead, spraying the area. For some moments they were pinned flat in the rough grass. He turned his head carefully and saw the winking muzzle flare of the gun in a tree near the clearing. He slammed a new magazine into the Uzi and fired deliberately in short, sharp bursts. There was a thrashing in the branches, a sudden scream, and then the Pao Thet's body hurtled down.

"Let's go."

He ran with Pala Mir for the parked Beechcraft. Men were running away across the airstrip now, caught between his own fire and the fire of the freed pilots, as well as the approaching forces of Colonel Tileong. He ignored them, searching the thick gloom for Hammond.

Suddenly he saw Hammond slipping through the brush to his left, making for the hangar sheds. The man was intent on his own business. As yet, there was no sign of Paul Merrydale. Maybe he had been caught in the village, but Durell did not think so. Paul would stay close to his plane.

"George!"

Hammond turned his head. His face was a death mask, gaunt and haggard, stained with mud and smoke. He motioned for Durell to stay back, but Durell ignored the signal and ran toward him. Hammond raised his gun, as if to warn him, but Pala Mir shouted something that was lost in the noise of the fighting nearby. Durell slid down the slope and skirted the long reed wall of the hangar. He could hear men in there, shouting to each other, and he was aware of the danger of explosions from the Thrashers' armaments. There came a rustle from his right and Hammond came up to lay beside him. Durell waved Pala Mir to cover them from a few yards above.

"Get her out of here," Hammond snapped. His breath came in hard, quick gasps. "I don't want her behind me."

"You can trust her. What are you after?"

"What do you think?" Hammond grinned. There were scratches on his face and blood on his left arm. "I'm getting Paul Merrydale's scalp. He'll make a break for his plane any second now, you'll see."

"I want him alive," Durell said. "He has to stand trial in Pasangara."

"Hell, no. You want this all over the world's newspapers? We'll wipe him."

"No," Durell said.

"You won't stop me."

Without further warning Hammond lurched up and raced for the hangar shed beside the airstrip, his gun blazing. There were shouts from inside, a scream, a burst of return fire.

Then Durell saw the familiar figure of Paul Merrydale break from a side door and run for the airstrip.

What followed was as inevitable as the approaching dark of night that was imminent. It was as if the demon that had driven Hammond this far in his single-minded purpose had arranged them all like puppets on a stage. There was no help for it, no turning back. Merrydale's tall figure and yellow hair were plain to identify in the flickering light of the distant fires. He carried a sub-machine gun as he ran for the plane, but Hammond's yell froze him for just an instant. Durrell saw Hammond raise his gun and drive at him, bowling him over, while Merrydale gasped and snarled, looking like a convulsed, enraged animal. He might have survived to stand trial in Pasangara if he had dropped his weapon then. But he spun away on his feet again, his back to the Beechcraft; his handsome face was almost unrecognizable in his fury. His machine gun came up and began to chatter, slamming slugs over Hammond's head and then swinging toward the line of prisoners running from the compound. In another instant they would have been blindly mown down by the man's rage.

The Rajah's heavy hunting rifle boomed just behind Durrell.

The single shot was like a punctuation to all the hammering of guns and grenades that had gone on for the last ten minutes.

Everything went silent.

Paul Merrydale slumped to his knees, dropping his smoking weapon. Hammond turned his head, calling out something to Durrell between his teeth, then walked back toward them. Behind Durrell, the Rajah said in a flat voice, "I could not let *him* do it, not really, I could not."

Shuddering, Pala Mir came to Durrell.

Merrydale was still on his knees, staring up at the tall figure of the White Rajah striding toward him. His face was anguished, mystified, not understanding.

"You, Grandpapa?"

"Yes."

Hammond made a whistling sound as his breath was sucked in. "I'd have done it for him. I wanted to do it. I had to do it. It was my job."

"Shut up, George."

Pala Mir shivered. "Is Paul dead?"

"Yes."

"It's over?"

"Not quite," said Durell. "Not quite over."

27

NOTHING had changed in the apartment over the Chinese herbalist's shop. The canal was quiet, mirroring the moon in its calm surface. The sound of gongs came from somewhere, along with the puttering of motorbikes and the tinkle of pedicab bells. Pasangara was quiet but sweltering under the tropical sun that blazed down over the South China Sea. The sampans had collected again around the bridge over the klong, and the smells of cooking and the sounds of chattering women came clearly on the warm night air.

Durell rested quietly on the big platform of the Chinese bed in the room that faced the klong. He had been waiting in the darkness for over an hour, as he had waited once before, and it seemed like an eternity. It was the second night since his return from the jungle.

He had seen David Condon and Premier Kuang. The roly-poly Kuang had visited the American consulate to formally express his regrets and appreciation, both at once, about the affair at the mountain palace. Arrangements had been made to ship the rescued Thrasher pilots back to their aircraft carrier. There had been no political difficulties. Everyone had been polite and formal, and not too many questions had been asked. Most of all, Durell thought, the big answer had not come up.

Colonel Tileong had lifted the curfew on the city. The

rioting was at an end, as abruptly as it had begun, and although racial enmity between Malay and Chinese still smoldered, Pasangara had every appearance of normality.

No one had reminded Durell that he had been ordered out of the province, a gesture for which he was mildly grateful. He was not finished here yet. He had spent a day sending coded messages via K Section's control at Kuala Lumpur, and two hours ago in Hammond's little basement office at the consulate, he had received his reply from General Dickinson McFee, who was flying from Taiwan to Washington tonight. Hammond had not been in the consulate then. Hammond had not been seen since their return to Pasangara.

Durell had tried to telephone to the waterfront palace and speak to Pala Mir. Anandara, the Indian woman, said quietly that the Rajah and his granddaughter were not seeing anyone. She was sorry. Perhaps in a few days, if Mr. Durell were still in Pasangara?

He did not expect to be in Pasangara after tomorrow night.

He still had the Walther P-38. Keeping two fingers on it as he lay on the Chinese bed, he listened to the bell of a pedicab as it went by. A Chinese woman was arguing with someone on a sampan across the way near the klong. The smells of cooking and canal mud drifted through the open window. Durell had kept the lights off, but after waiting patiently, he now began to wonder if he were too late. In some ways he wished he were. He envied his boss, McFee, on his flight over the Pacific back to the States.

The apartment furnishings loomed in heavy dark teak around him. The bed was comfortable. He wished he could sleep. He felt the heavy, oily metal of the gun beside him on the bed and watched lights move across the ceiling as a car went by. It was a Renault; he could tell by the sound of the engine. The car paused near the edge of the klong and the motor ran for another moment or two. Then the car started up again, and the normal sounds of the night resumed.

It was difficult to believe that an insane massacre had raged in the city only a few days before.

All of a sudden he heard the very faint creak of the stairs. The steps had been soundless before, but he had worked with screwdriver and chisel, loosening one tread, testing it again and again until he was sure it would sound a warning when a man's weight rested on it.

Durell lay still, closing his hand on the gun.

Hammond came into the apartment. He made no attempt to conceal his entrance now. The end of his small, crooked Dutch cigar made a red glow in the darkness as he opened the door with a key and then closed it meticulously. His shadow was tall and lean, tilted a little to one side to favor his injured leg. He wore a rumpled seersucker suit with a thin, black string tie and a white Thai silk shirt.

"Cajun?"

"Here," Durell said.

"You like my bed?"

"I'd like to sleep in it for a week."

"You keep surprising me like this, and you might sleep in it forever. I don't like unexpected visitors."

"You've been expecting me, George. Haven't you?"

Hammond's big teeth gleamed. "Yes, I have."

"Then you're not surprised."

"No. I know all about you, Cajun. You like everything tied up in neat packages, pretty bow, string and all. But our business doesn't end that way."

"It will," Durell said. "Where've you been?"

"Busy. Out and around. Is it okay for a light?"

"We don't need one," Durell said.

Hammond peered. "You throwing a gun on me, Cajun?"

"I figured you have strange visitors. It happened the last time with Lily Fan."

Hammond sat down in a chair facing the bed; Durell sat up, cross-legged, and rested the gun on his knee. He did not point it at anything in particular. Out in the harbor a freighter hooted. The hot night wind brought the sound of Buddhist temple bells from somewhere in the city.

A silence rested between them. Hammond dragged at his cigar, and the red glow lit up the seams of his face, his scar, the heavy gray brows, the thick hair that seemed all white now. His eyes under the brows were dark, careful pools of watching and waiting.

Finally, Hammond said, "All right, get it off your chest. You didn't like the way I handled my piece of the action. You don't have to like it, Cajun. I'm the control in Pasangara. You're supposed to take orders from me. You didn't. And I've sent a prejudicial report to K Section to that effect. If that makes you sore at me, too bad. I don't think we'll work with each other again."

"No, I'm sure we won't."

"I expect I'll be called back to Washington for doing this job. Maybe I'll get back into the middle of things. I did admit," Hammond said quietly, "that you were something of a help. Both a help and a hindrance. I didn't need you and I didn't want you here. I had the Thrashers located and I had Paul spotted. It was just a question of getting through the riot curfew and cleaning it up."

"So you plan to leave Pasangara, George?"

"Hell, yes." His tone was smug and pleased. "I've waited a long time for a break like this. A comeback, if you will. A chance to prove I've still got it. Hell, the business is my life. I was dying here."

"You had Lily Fan," Durell said.

"Oh, well. . . ." The cigar made an arc in the darkness, a gesture of dismissal.

"I thought you wanted to marry the girl."

"You know how it is when a man gets frustrated and lonely, away from the action."

"I hear Premier Kuang has taken her back into his personal custody. A question of her being too young and simply out for excitement."

"Yes," Hammond said.

"Have you seen her since we got back?"

"No."

"I have," said Durell.

"Well, she was a pretty piece."

"Then why were you so anxious to kill her, George?"

There was a silence. Hammond sighed, then answered, "Get it off your mind, Cajun." His voice had changed very subtly, hardening just a little.

"That's what I'm here for, George."

"Listen, I used Lily Fan to find out what was going on in the premier's office. She was—she is—his favorite daughter. He'll forget and forgive her affair with me. It was my business to get information, right? My business was to know what goes on in Pasangara. Premier Kuang wasn't about to hand me the data I wanted, but Lily got it all for me whenever I asked. It was as simple as that."

"I think not," Durell said. "You broke every rule in the book with her. You were crazy about her. You were out of your mind with lust for her. But you wanted to kill her. You didn't make it out there, but you managed to get Paul Merrydale out of the way. You managed to get that poor old man, the Rajah, to kill his own grandson. A break for you. But it didn't matter with me. Either way you were out to kill Paul and silence him."

"So I hate traitors and Commies," Hammond said.

"Do you hate yourself?" Durell asked.

Hammond leaned forward in the chair and silently tapped the ash off his cigar. Light flickered across the ceiling. As Hammond moved, Durell swung his legs off the huge Chinese bed and sat up, the Walther in his lap resting on his right thigh. There was the puttering sound of a motorbike outside along the canal, and when it faded, Durell heard Hammond's breath sigh softly again.

"I guess you'd better explain that one, Cajun."

"If I have to."

"You'd better."

"I'm sorry for you, George," said Durell.

There was a quickly stifled note of impatient exasperation in the other's voice. "I'm tired of people being sorry for me. I'm tired of sitting here at the end of the world, wasting myself. Everything I know I can do damned well, damned better than you. Don't say that again."

Durell watched Hammond's hands.

Hammond drew on his cigar. "Everything here is cleaned up. I don't know what you're after, Cajun. We found the Thrashers, we got the pilots out, they're on their way home to R & R and a fat bonus in their pay. Okay, so the old Rajah had to shoot his grandson. Good for him. He had guts. That crappy Paul was going to mow down the pilots we went in to save, wasn't he? He was trying to escape in his private plane. He could've made it to Cambodia, anywhere. You say I wanted to kill him. But the way it turned out, I didn't, did I? What are you sore about?"

"I don't like double agents," Durell said.

Hammond said softly, "Meaning me?"

"You tried to play both ends against the middle, George. When it started, when the Pao Thets began their killing around here, you thought you were at the end of the line, buried in Pasangara, not trusted any more by K Section. But you've always been a security man to your fingertips. You saw a chance for a new career. Was it Paul who first approached you? Made a fat offer for you to work for the Pao Thets as their intelligence chief? Granted, Paul got the Boomerangs and thought up the whole idea of luring our planes down here, guiding them in as a Judas pilot, using them, hopefully, to bomb the city and set up a smoke screen for international propaganda. Then, during the confusion you'd take over the whole province. Paul was ambitious. He rode his old grandfather hard when the Rajah still pretended to have some authority here from the old days. Paul wanted that authority back; he wanted to run Pasangara as the White Rajahs had once done—only, this time, under a red flag, perhaps as a Red Rajah. Paul wanted to prove himself just as you wanted to—but you both went off in the wrong direction."

"Speaking of proof——" Hammond began.

"I don't have any," Durell admitted.

"Then stop talking yourself into the grave, Cajun."

"I won't, buddy-wuddy."

Hammond sat very still. "Ah."

"You used Lily Fan to get information out of her father's office, right out of Premier Kuang's files. She was just a silly girl who climbed into bed with you, whom you glamorized into thinking you were something important. For a time, I thought Lily was working with Paul, that maybe she was really Paul's woman. I didn't know. But you were using her. You've been in the business too long. You're too old, George, to flip over a younger woman the way you pretended. I didn't buy it. I never did."

Durell paused. "You tried to kill me when I went to save Pala Mir that night in the canal right here. You tried to kill me several times on the way to the mountain. Every booby trap you left had your trademark on it, George. The bridge, the dranghs, the trip wire in the cave that could have dropped a rock on my skull.

"You were afraid Lily Fan might convince me of the truth when she got away from you. And when you got your hands on her again, you gagged her, saying she might alert the Pao Thets. But what you really wanted was to keep her quiet. The same thing went for Paul Merrydale. You weren't worried about the pilots' lives. You just wanted to shut Paul's mouth, knowing he was really weak, knowing he would babble all about your part in the Pao Thet insurgency. You did your damnedest to kill him before I could reach him, and it worked out pretty well for you, except for one thing."

"Yes?" Hammond asked.

"You sent Parepa with me with orders to kill me. You weren't sure how much I knew or suspected. But Parepa picked up the phrase buddy-wuddy from you and used it, giving himself away."

It was quiet in the room now. Hammond didn't move in his chair, except to raise the cigar to his mouth. The smoke curled through the darkness and touched Durell's nostrils. Durell inhaled deeply.

"Go ahead."

"I knew it wasn't Paul who was the Judas pilot all the time. It had to be someone else sometimes, flying alternate nights. The first time I heard a Thrasher go over, Paul was right there with Pala Mir at her river house. But you weren't in Pasangara; you were gone all day. It's just a short flight in the Beechcraft, just an hour from the mountain to the city. I checked you out, George. You can fly a Thrasher better than most. You had jet training in '64, for the Kurd project you ran in Syria. There were two Judas pilots who lured the Navy planes down here—Paul and you."

Hammond kept silent.

"You still saw a chance to come out of it all right," Durell added, "even after I arrived. If you could scrub Paul and Lily Fan, you'd be a hero to K Section, right back on top where you wanted to be. It was the chance you'd been waiting for, for years. Either way, with us or them, you thought you'd win. If you could kill me, you could still play the other side of the coin and run things with Paul and the Pao Thets. If not, you were right back in K Section. You wanted to have your cake and eat it, too." Durell sighed. "But you can't, George. I won't let you."

"Have you reported all this?" Hammond asked softly.

"Yes, I have."

Hammond inhaled his cigar and blew the smoke out with a soft hissing sound. His voice was calm. "If it didn't work, I figured I'd be back in K Section as a hero, great old George, a real tiger. And if it did work, I'd be running things in Pasangara. A Red Rajah, as you say. It seemed pretty good to me. I've been out in the boonies too long to retire, Cajun. They'll do the same thing to you one day."

"Perhaps."

"Have you had any return orders about me?"

"Yes," Durell said. "You are to be eliminated, as the office says, with extreme prejudice."

Hammond was silent for a moment.

"Tough on you, Cajun," he said.

"Yes."

"You don't want to do it."

"But I will."

"Yeah. I know you will. Anyway, you'll try." Hammond sat quietly for a long moment. Then he stood up and limped across the darkly shadowed room, stared at the window, stared at the muzzle of Durell's gun that had followed his every move. The cigar end glowed redly again. He said quietly, "We're all fools, playing a fool's game. We think we know what we're doing, but somebody else is always pulling the strings. I guess the loneliness here, the kind of exile it's been for me—through no fault of my own, I might add—made me go a bit wiggy. I felt it was an injustice, Cajun. I've always been the same man I was before they got to me in East Germany."

"Not quite," Durell said.

"Maybe not for a little time. But lately—"

"Lately you've been working for them, not us."

Hammond took the cigar from his mouth and stared at it. Durell could see no expression in the dark pools of his eyes.

"I'll save you the trouble, Sam," he said quietly. "I could take you, I think, even with your gun on me. But I'd have no place to go after that. And I don't want to hurt you, Cajun. It's the job, the business, that makes us stay here in this room and do what we're doing to each other. All of a sudden, I'm sick of it. I'm tired. I've lost. I hope some day if it ever gets to be your turn, you get a break, Sam. I hope so but it won't happen."

Hammond put the cigar in his mouth, showed his teeth in a strange smile, and then bit down savagely on the end of it.

Durell heard the crunch of the poison capsule in the tip of the cigar. He didn't move.

A minute later, Hammond was dead.

28

THE Kuan Diop Hotel had returned to normal the evening after Hammond's death. Durell had spent the day at the consulate with David Condon, filing and encoding his last reports, arranging for the transfer of the Navy pilots and the planes back up north. He had received a brief interview with Premier Kuang in which polite formality prevailed. Lily Fan was being sent off to school. Nothing was said about Durell's presence at the guerrilla mountain headquarters, and only murmured regrets were expressed about Hammond's death.

Colonel Tileong called at the hotel and was more specific. Durell told him as little as possible. Durell inquired about the Rajah and was informed that the old gentleman had barred himself in his dilapidated waterfront palace and was seeing no one.

"It is a tragedy," Tileong said gently. His brown face was bland. "We in Pasangara are all very fond of him. He had high hopes of his grandson's becoming a political presence, so to speak, in the province. But, of course, that would never have been permitted."

"I understand," Durell nodded.

"As for my lieutenant, Parepa—I understand you were with him when he died?"

"A brave man, Colonel."

"Ah, yes. Ambitious as well, I always thought." Tileong paused. "We have listed his death as being at the hands of the Pao Thets. He died bravely. Now the city is calm, eh? One does not stir the caldron without need, eh?"

Durell murmured something, and Tileong asked when

he would be leaving. Durell told him it would be the next
day, then asked about Pala Mir.

"She is with the Rajah. I doubt very much if she will
allow any visitors, Mr. Durell." Tileong's brown eyes
understood him. "You are fond of her, and she has been
much maligned. A pity she has no one to console her."

Durell was in his shower when he heard the rap on his
hotel room door. It was past nine in the evening, and he
had ordered a bottle of bourbon from the bar downstairs,
which was crowded as usual with Chinese, Dutch, English,
and Indian merchants. He was looking at the prospect of
a solitary evening with some sleep until nine in the morning, when a shuttle plane would take him to Kuala Lumpur and then onward to the States. But it was not a
skirted hotel servant who appeared in the corridor when
he opened the door.

Pala Mir stood there.

She smiled.

"Hello, Sam."

"Hello."

"May I come in?"

"Of course."

He was conscious of his worn, gray bathrobe, his wet
hair. She was dressed in a silver sari trimmed with violet,
and she wore a narrow diadem of amethysts that matched
the colors embroidered on the sari. Silver slippers were
on her feet. Her peach skin was without makeup; she
needed none. The slight tilt of her Eurasian eyes crinkled
with faint amusement.

"Weren't you expecting me, Sam?"

"Frankly, no."

"I came on behalf of the Rajah. He regrets the necessity that forced him to do—what he did, about Paul."

Durell said, "But Paul was your twin brother."

"Grandpapa always said that Paul was the evil half of
me. If that implies that I am good—" She shrugged and
smiled. "I think I'm not. I do not mourn Paul, you see.
What he did was barbarous, the worst treachery against

all of us in Pasangara." She paused. "Do you mourn Mr. Hammond, Sam?"

"In some ways."

"Yes . . . You look uncomfortable, Sam."

He was aware of his dripping figure, the old robe. "I was just—alone," he said. "Waiting for my plane, tomorrow."

"In something like twelve hours," she murmured. "You will really leave then?"

"I must."

"Twelve hours can be a lifetime," Pala Mir said. "I seem to be overdressed for the occasion."

She did something to the silver sari, and it came apart in a heap at her feet. Then, smiling, she walked toward him.

Durell turned off the lights.

ENJOY THE OTHER SAM DURELL ADVENTURES

ASSIGNMENT—

ANKARA   R2056   60¢
BLACK VIKING   D1823   50¢
BUDAPEST   R2040   60¢
THE CAIRO DANCERS   D1983   50¢
CARLOTTA CORTEZ   R2088   60¢
CONG HAI KILL   R2011   60¢
THE GIRL IN THE GONDOLA   R2054   60¢
LOWLANDS   R2028   60¢

A Fawcett   Gold Medal Book

Wherever Paperbacks Are Sold

IN THE BESTSELLING "ASSIGNMENT" SERIES

ASSIGNMENT—

MADELEINE   D1950   50¢

MARA TIRANA   D1920   50¢

MOON GIRL   R2024   60¢

NUCLEAR NUDE   R2000   60¢

PEKING   R2145   60¢

SCHOOL FOR SPIES   R1999   60¢

SUICIDE   D1944   50¢

SULU SEA   D1967   50¢

TREASON   D1958   50¢

ZORAYA   R2071   60¢

A Fawcett Gold Medal Book

Wherever Paperbacks Are Sold

If your bookdealer is sold out, send cover price plus 10¢ each for postage and handling to Gold Medal Books, Fawcett Publications, Inc., Greenwich, Conn. 06830. If order is for five or more books, there is no postage or handling charge. Order by number and title. No Canadian orders.

By the creator of the "ASSIGNMENT" series

Edward S. Aarons
PASSAGE TO TERROR

The passage to terror is exactly that—the story of
an innocent guy named Pete Cole, fleeing to Central
America with the exotic Serafina as his guide. But
Serafina was up to her beautiful eyes in a web of
intrigue—and every time she put her arms around
Pete, he wondered where her knife would strike.

Edward S. Aarons ". . . knows how to tell a fast professional story of double agents and triple treachery."

—*The New York Times*